Theatre and Moral Order

Volume 15

Published by the

Southeastern Theatre Conference and

The University of Alabama Press

THEATRE SYMPOSIUM is published annually by the Southeastern Theatre Conference, Inc. (SETC), and by The University of Alabama Press. SETC nonstudent members receive the journal as a part of their membership under rules determined by SETC. For information on membership write to SETC, P.O. Box 9868, Greensboro, NC 27429-0868. All other inquiries regarding subscriptions, circulation, purchase of individual copies, and requests to reprint materials should be addressed to The University of Alabama Press, Box 870380, Tuscaloosa, AL 35487-0380.

THEATRE SYMPOSIUM publishes works of scholarship resulting from a single-topic meeting held on a southeastern university campus each spring. A call for papers to be presented at that meeting is widely publicized each autumn for the following spring. Authors are encouraged to send unsolicited manuscripts directly to the editor. Information about the next symposium is available from the editor, Jay Malarcher, Division of Theatre and Dance, College of Creative Arts, West Virginia University, P.O. Box 6111, Morgantown, WV 26506-6111, jay.malarcher@mail.wvu.edu

THEATRE SYMPOSIUM
A PUBLICATION OF THE SOUTHEASTERN THEATRE CONFERENCE

Volume 15 — Contents — *2007*

Introduction	5
Don't Let What Really Happened Get in the Way of the Truth: Reflections on Theatre, Ethics, and "The Moral Order" Rosemarie K. Bank	8
What Moral Order? Observations from the Trenches Steve Scott	20
William Dunlap, Father of American Theatre—and American Antitheatricality David Carlyon	29
"NOT from the Drowsy Pulpit!" The Moral Reform Melodrama on the Nineteenth-Century Stage John W. Frick	41
Tainted Money? Nineteenth-Century Charity Theatricals Eileen Curley	52
The Doomed Courtesan and Her Moral Reformers Rachel Rusch	74
Gender and (Im)morality in Restoration Comedy: Aphra Behn's *The Feigned Courtesans* Leah Lowe	92
Solving the *Laramie* Problem, or, Projecting onto *Laramie* Roger Freeman	107

4 CONTENTS

The Advantage of Controversy: *Angels in America* and Campus Culture Wars   123
   James Fisher

Excerpt from the Symposium Response   133
   Steve Scott

Contributors   137

Introduction

In April of 2006 Atlanta's Agnes Scott College hosted the fifteenth annual SETC Theatre Symposium. The focus of the gathering was theatre and the moral order, a broadly defined topic that drew more than thirty-five participants from throughout the United States, Canada, and Europe. The purpose of the gathering was to investigate how, historically, the theatre has been perceived as a focus of moral anxiety or, conversely, as an instrument of moral and social reform.

These two perceptions of the stage—the one grounded in neo-Platonic anxieties about the putative moral dangers inherent in performance itself, the other in the Aristotelian celebration of the utopian possibilities and regenerative potential of theatrical "instruction"—form a familiar trope repeated by critics throughout history, from Plato, Tertullian, William Prynne, and Jessie Helms at one pole to Aristotle, Moliere, Henry Irving, and Hallie Flanagan on the other.

Theatre and Moral Order begins with essays by our two distinguished keynoters, Professor Rosemarie K. Bank of Kent State University, author of *Theatre Culture in America, 1825–1860,* and Steve Scott, actor, director, and associate producer at Chicago's Tony Award–winning Goodman Theatre. In "Don't Let What Really Happened Get in the Way of the Truth: Reflections on Theatre, Ethics, and 'The Moral Order,'" Professor Bank considers George Catlin's Indian Gallery (1844); Buffalo Bill's engagement at the Columbian Exposition of 1893; and other ethnographic depictions of the savage "other," the moral ramifications of "staging" the "native," and, as she puts it, "the power of the ungenuine, the fictive, the performative to be more true than the true." Written from the viewpoint of a professional theatre practitioner,

Scott's "What Moral Order? Observations from the Trenches" grapples with the moral function of theatre in an increasingly fragmented world where any notion of *a* moral order has been replaced by multiple moral and ethical codes.

The following three essays are concerned with the early American stage as a vehicle for social and cultural reform. Dave Carlyon looks at the surprisingly antitheatrical impulses of William Dunlap, the "Father of the American Theatre," while John Frick examines the sometimes complicated relationship between the so-called moral reform melodrama and the broader reformist ideologies and movements of the nineteenth century. For the producers of moral reform melodrama the stage was a place for the fruitful intersection of commercial interests and social consciousness (albeit not always seamless), whereas for Dunlap the stage is a place where practitioners must remain vigilant against the theatre's own worst impulses and excesses. Eileen Curley looks at the ways in which organizers of charity theatricals negotiated standards of middle-class respectability (particularly with regard to women) even as the lines between the socially acceptable amateur stage and the morally ambiguous professional world became increasingly blurred in the late nineteenth century. Curley's article reminds us that moral ambiguity has fallen hardest on women and, certainly within the canon of Western dramatic literature, on "fallen women."

Rachel Rusch tracks the doomed courtesan—specifically the paradigmatic character of Marguerite Gautier—as she becomes a barometer of the constantly shifting ground of late nineteenth- and early twentieth-century moral and sexual discourse. In her treatment of Aphra Behn's *The Feigned Courtesans* Leah Lowe demonstrates the ways in which Behn, the first professional female playwright of the English-speaking world, collapses the traditional binary of virgin/prostitute and creates a liminal space in which "feminine sexual self-determination" subverts Restoration patriarchal norms.

Next the collection offers two essays linked to what has in recent years been loosely termed "the culture wars." Roger Freeman looks at the disjunction between text and performance in two productions of *The Laramie Project,* particularly the ways in which these productions impose an extratextual moral gloss on what Freeman considers a morally "neutral" text. The final essay is Jim Fisher's personal memoir of the controversy surrounding his production of Tony Kushner's *Angels in America.* Fisher, one of the country's foremost Kushner scholars, recounts the attempt by officials at one of the nation's prominent liberal arts colleges to censor a theatre production, a chilling reminder that the academic and artistic freedom so many of us in the academy take for granted is far from a sure thing in the current American atmosphere of moral and political polarization. The volume concludes with a conference response by Steve Scott, whose perspective as a professional director, actor, and producer provide vital insight into the intersections of theory, criticism, and practice.

I have many people to thank for the successful completion of this volume: associate editor Jay Malarcher, who will assume the editorship of this series next year, for assisting with the symposium event, for vetting submissions, and for editing the conference response; former *Symposium* editors Phil Hill and Susan Kattwinkel for their advice and support; Dan Waterman and the entire staff at the University of Alabama Press for their uncompromising professionalism and efficient management of the project from initial manuscript to finished volume; Southeastern Theatre Conference president Dennis Wemm and executive director Betsey Baun for their ongoing support of this series and SETC's continued promotion of theatre scholarship. Thanks also to the Auburn University Department of Theatre for its logistical support of my efforts, particularly to department chair Dan Larocque, for his indulgence in allowing me the time to complete this volume, and to Linda Bell, for her assistance with the cover photo.

Finally, I must express my gratitude to David Thompson, who made it possible to hold the symposium gathering on the campus of Agnes Scott College. Thank you, David; you and your students were consummate hosts, and I greatly appreciate your efforts.

SCOTT PHILLIPS
AUBURN UNIVERSITY

Don't Let What Really Happened Get in the Way of the Truth

Reflections on Theatre, Ethics, and "The Moral Order"

Rosemarie K. Bank

IT SEEMS ALTOGETHER APPROPRIATE that this address comes toward the middle of a conference called "Theatre and the Moral Order"—neither a keynote sounded at the beginning of things, like a paean signaling a battle charge, nor an endnote, echoing, at the finish, the matter sounded throughout—appropriate because, while "the moral" is always of the moment, "the moral order" is retrospective. In "The Storyteller," Walter Benjamin draws the relationship between the two as that between the perpetuating remembrance and the reminiscence that expresses it. Since, in my view, moral orders are constructs, not "facts," we need to address that larger thing, the ethical—the principles and rules of which the "right conduct" or "customs" of the moral are the reflection—from which moral orders (the performances of those principles and rules) are constructed. Though we can already see "the moral" as an acting out, a performance of what I elsewhere call theatre culture, a middle position lets us look back from the space of the now, toward a beginning that has already begun, and ahead to an endgame that has not yet been played, to triangulate a discourse too often positioned in such binary terms as *then* and *now* or *good* and *evil*. In the midst of things we will move from ethics to theatre and back to ethics, with stops in the history of the American (septentrional) and U.S. theatre. I have in view the story of (theatre) history reflected in a National Public Radio broadcast I recently heard in which the storyteller spoke of an incident that happened to him in the sixth grade (or such), which he had reminisced in his writing into a tale at some remove from "what really happened." Inevitably, the day came when he told the tale to an audience that had in it one of his sixth-grade classmates. Certain of the exposure and rebuke that must inevitably follow his perversion of "the truth," the storyteller braced himself as the audience member confronted him—and effused that the storyteller had perfectly captured the incident and accurately remembered the details after so many years. Let us see what we may think of our (hi)stories when, as Theodor Adorno observes in *Minima Moralia,* "The ungenuineness of the genuine stems from its need to claim, in a society dominated by exchange, to be what it stands for yet is never able to be." The beginning, then, has begun.[1]

Three ancient words reverberate in the consideration of "ethics" as a contemporary construct: *ethikós* = of morals, *ethnikós* (from *éthnos* = nation), and *ethos* = character (in the moral sense—and we can readily connect *ethos* to ethics/*ethikós*). When the Greeks began to classify types of knowing—the dialectic (primarily philosophical) from the rhetorical (primarily political) from the aesthetic (primarily beautiful), and so on—they did so in the context of *logos,* the Greek word for speech,

> an ambiguous and sometimes mystical concept which may refer concretely to a word, words, or an entire oration, or may be used abstractly to indicate the meaning behind a word or expression or the power of thought and organization or the rational principle of the universe or the will of God. On the human level it involves man's thought and his function in society, and it further includes artistic creativity and the power of personality.[2]

Our own less-elastic language drives a wedge between what is said and what is done at the same time that it glides silently across the abyss separating thought and deed, as in these definitions of *ethics* from my dictionary: "the principles of morality, including both the science of the good and the nature of the right; the rules of conduct recognized in respect to a particular class of human actions; the science of the human character in its ideal state." It seems, then, that "ethics refers to rules and standards of conduct and practice," and morals "to generally accepted customs of conduct and right living in a society, and to the individual's practice in relation to these."[3]

"Moral order" attempts to legislate the distance between principle and practice in a manner akin to definitions of the word *duty,* rules of conduct writ large, papering over the gap Benjamin marks between remembrance (of one hero, one odyssey, one battle) and reminiscence (of many lives, common journeys, repeated struggles), the stuff of *ethnikós,* the ethnic or national. One example of "what really happened" getting in the way of "the truth"—the one to the many, the ethic to the ethnic—finds vivid expression in Louis-Armand de Lom d'Arce, Baron de Lahontan's *Nouveaux voyages... dans l'Amérique* (1703), an account of soldier/explorer/agent Lahontan's travels in Canada between 1683 and 1693. The third part of this book consists of "a satiric dialogue between Lahontan and a Huron interlocutor named Adario," a dramatization inserted into an "authentic" travel narrative that "contains virtually all the modes of colonial American secular writing: exploration narrative, historical accounts of Indian wars, natural history, description of the geography and economy of the colony, promotion and criticism of its potential, ethnography or *mours des sauvages,* and a glossary of a native language." Though secular writing, *Nouveaux voyages* recounts Lahontan's transformation from Frenchman to American as the result of his two winters hunting and living with groups of Algonquin Indians in Canada and the area around Detroit. What he experienced and recalls in his narrative is the free movement and action of the inhabitants, so unlike European prohibitions against hunting the seigneur's land, felling trees, building at will, and the like.[4]

The principle of freedom and equality displayed by the North Americans would become part of the ideology of the United States, the Adario dialogue serving as one "native" source among many for the reflection of these ideas in U.S. foundational oratory and documents—and Lahontan is and was the best known of all New France writers to students of French literature, Thomas Jefferson, John Adams, and Benjamin Franklin among them. Of course, Lahontan had European motives for crafting Adario, who, the narrative tells us, has been to France, so he can offer a comparative perspective to the Frenchman he regards as the slave of authority, class, and tradition, a man without the personal freedom Adario enjoys to refuse to fight another man's war, to say what he thinks, to live and hunt where he will, and to challenge and refuse to obey those who would set themselves above him. Purportedly based on a Huron named Kondiaronk, Adario is a hybrid challenge to colonial assumptions about North American savagism that forces a reading of history through story, since historical or ethnohistorical "fact" in travel narratives cannot be divided from fabulated evidence, a moment when "truth" gets in the way of "what really happened" and "what really happened" in the way of "the truth." Ethic and ethnic blend to project the moral order derived from the *mours des sauvages* in our corner of the theatre of ideas as well, that is, in the theatrical construction of the noble savage. Lahontan's Adario stands as prologue to Robert Rogers's *Ponteach* (1766) and Chateaubriand's Chactas (1801, from the latter's *Atala; or, The Loves of Two Savages in the Desert*), and the U.S. Indian plays that flourished in the antebellum decades of the nineteenth century.[5]

In 1976 Hayden White declared, "The theme of the Noble Savage may be one of the few historical topics about which there is nothing more to say." Binarized moral orders—noble savage/ruthless savage—take comfort in having said all there is to say about thought that, as Michel Foucault conceives it, incessantly thinks itself, thought that claims (Adorno again) "to be what it stands for yet is never able to be," a history above "all that," proposing a newer, better, and always clearer moral order, erasing the ambiguity of speech to reinsert "the rational principle of the universe or the will of God." Since, in White's mode, we cannot know "what really happened," Adario may make no truth claim; he has, simply, "nothing more to say" and must be silent, for, in this view, there is no "truth" except in "what really happened" in the binarized world of then and now, of good and evil. This is the world of moral orders, legislating the distance between principle and practice and our duty in remembering the Other.[6]

Adario's *logos* escapes binarized discourse to triangulate the trope of the noble/ruthless savage by creating a third thing, which is the product of cultural exchange. In this view, *noble* is not the opposite of *ruthless* but its twin; that is, to use Hegel's terminology, each is the sublation of the other, now releasing now suppressing the contradiction each trope presents to the other. It is an ambiguity and inconsistency wholly evident in the many Indian dramas that descend from Adario and from other models for the role of noble or ruthless savage, each of which is colored by views of what I have elsewhere identified (after Gordon Sayre) as the *sauvage* (the wild, natural, or rugged—still the first definition of savage in my dictionary) and the savage (the barbarous, uncivilized, or cruel). On the one hand, then, as historian Richard Slotkin observes of William Smith's 1765 *Historical Account* of the French and Indian War, "the proper way to live in America is to imitate the Indian, and . . . the Indian's patriotism, independence, and love of liberty make him the model of the ideal American." This Indian is a cruel and effective fighter—killing from ambush, relentless in eliminating his enemies, merciless in replenishing his stores from his enemy's larder while denying them to his foe—*and* a selfless, loyal patriot who honors courage and dedication in others. Speaking beyond the limits of White's closed discourse, Gordon Sayre observes that "the vision of the Indian was always bound up with the colonists' ideas of what kind of society they wished to create," a "colonist who internalizes the Indian he demonizes" and finds nobility "in the successful synthesis of oppositions."[7]

I want, briefly, to identify two more instances of the interaction of *ethikós* and *ethnikós* in the research I have in hand before I return to history writing and the moral order, briefly because I have discussed these instances elsewhere, and, though I've been working on the project of which they form a part for over a decade, they are thoughts in danger of incessantly speaking (if not thinking) themselves. The two instances involve a visit to George Catlin's Indian Gallery, and the idea of museumized history, and Buffalo Bill's Wild West at the end of the nineteenth century, which is where my project ends. (More contemporary settings will come into the discussion of historiography and the moral order, with which this episode of the story will end.)[8]

George Catlin was born in 1796 and lived in upstate New York and in Pennsylvania at a time when Indian people, living tribally, were resident there. He experienced something of an epiphany when he saw a delegation of Indians passing through Philadelphia while he was studying art in the city, and he began to paint Indians, the Seneca leader Red Jacket in 1826 and Winnebago delegates encountered in Washington in the fall of 1828. Catlin knew the art gallery and natural history museum operated by the American painter and Philosophical Society regular Charles Willson Peale, housed on the upper floors of Independence Hall in Philadelphia, an institution that came to incorporate live acts and exhibits and played an active role in American history (an Indian delegation purportedly concluded an impromptu peace treaty at Peale's Museum in 1796, when it accidentally encountered a rival tribe there while both were on tour to the seat of power). The priceless artifacts in Peale's prestigious museum—from mastodon bones from Pennsylvania to the goods collected by Lewis and Clarke on their 1804–6 expedition—would ultimately fall into the hands of Phineas T. Barnum's American Museum in New York and Moses Kimball's Boston Museum, each of which operated a theatre, as Peale's heirs would come to do. The delegation Catlin saw inspired him to become a "history" painter of Indians before they (in his view) passed from the scene. Catlin set out for St. Louis in 1830 and traveled the trans-Mississippi West intermittently until 1836, sketching and painting Indians and scenes from Indian life, recording Indian ceremonies, and gathering hundreds of Indian artifacts.[9]

In the fall of 1837, Catlin began to exhibit his Indian Gallery in New York and, in 1838, in Washington, DC. The Indian Gallery consisted of the paintings made from Catlin's trips and the materials he had collected during his travels exhibited in the context of performance and enactment. The Crow teepee he had acquired on his travels served as the centerpiece for a lecture illustrated by paintings, clothing, musical instruments, weapons, jewelry, and other artifacts. When Catlin exhibited in New York, prominent citizens were invited to eat a collation of buffalo's tongue inside the teepee, smoke the pipes, wear the clothing, listen to Catlin's experiences in the West and, hopefully, buy his paintings. Failing to secure a purchaser for the entire collection in the United States, Catlin moved his gallery to London in 1840, where his nephew and a troupe of Cockney men and boys illustrated the lectures and paintings by masquerading as Indians and performing war dances and other "Indian acts" at regularly scheduled performances. In 1843 the first of three troupes of Indian performers, nine Ojibway men and women, under the management of Canadian showman Arthur Rankin, joined Catlin's Indian Gallery. In 1844 a party of sixteen Iowa, recruited by Barnum, replaced them, and a successful tour of England and France ensued, during which three of the Iowa died. The third troupe, eleven Ojibway Indians who had been touring England successfully under their own management, connected with Catlin in London, and the Indian Gallery began a second tour of Europe in 1845, where a smallpox epidemic overtook them.[10]

Catlin's Indian Gallery did not cast Indians, real or false, as noble or ruthless savages but offered a performative version of *mœurs des sauvages* instead. Accordingly, the show was divided into male and female activities, the latter "descriptive of Domestic Scenes in Indian life in times of peace; representing their Games—Dances—Feasts—Marriage Ceremonies—Funeral Rites—Mysteries, etc.," and tailored for family audiences and women, and the former consisting of war dances, skulking, a scalp dance, a pipe of peace dance, and the like, intended for visitors drawn to the more robust melodramatic fare of the day. Catlin's Indian Gallery offered museumized entertainment as a form of ethnographic instruction: the Indians were (ultimately) Indians, the customs were (transplanted) Indian customs, but, as in a museum, everything was out-of-place and contextualized by nonnatives. Moreover, since Catlin believed the Indian subjects of his paintings were vanishing, his Indian Gallery was staged in the colors of the past rather than the present. Although Catlin took the Indians sightseeing, for example, both for their sake and so they would be seen and draw visitors to the Indian Gallery, they traveled in attention-getting regalia rather than in the effacing western clothing they also wore. (In the same vein Catlin, earlier, had attended public balls in London with a white Indian agent impersonating an Indian in his gallery.) Taking the Iowa for exercise at Lord's cricket ground and encamping them at Vauxhall Gardens, after their run at Egyptian Hall ended in 1844, Catlin added the effects of popular equestrian performances to the instruction provided by the *mœurs des sauvages* of earlier travel narratives, such as Lahontan's *Nouveaux voyages*.[11]

Given the fascination with "the Other" that characterizes the nineteenth century, it has not been difficult for later historians to adopt an antitheatrical stance toward exhibiting and performing "the Indian." In this view, Indian cultures are denigrated by white reminiscences of them, and Indian performers are the exploited dupes of theatrical managers or museum exhibitors. Rather than this binary and its legislation of the distance between twentieth-century principle and nineteenth-century practice, historians have re-membered Buffalo Bill's Wild West and the ceremony of memory and celebrity it represents. While George Catlin was not averse to playing Indian, William F. Cody devoted his performative life to playing Buffalo Bill, an identity located in what the Bureau of Indian Affairs in the 1890s called "show Indians" and we call professional performers. Even the generous time allotted an address of this sort is hardly enough to sketch more than a point or two about Cody's work as actor and manager that speak to the text of theatre, ethics, and the moral order. My point of intersection—no surprise here—will be Buffalo Bill's Wild West and Congress of Rough Riders of the World at the Columbian Exposition of 1893.[12]

The show that Buffalo Bill and his comanager, Nate Salsbury, stapled to the flank of the Columbian Exposition in Chicago, when they were denied a space on the fairground itself, had developed over the years from such immediate progenitors as a show by Brulé Sioux that Cody put together in 1872, in his days as an army scout, for a frontier tour by Grand Duke Alexis, son of the Russian czar, that involved feats of arms, horsemanship, dancing, drumming, and singing. Boosted by published stories and his own memoir of his exploits as a scout and buffalo hunter, Cody attempted to start an acting career in such thinly derived plays as the 1872 *Scouts of the Prairie,* but it was the adoption of the equestrian show format, beginning in 1883, that led to the success of Buffalo Bill's Wild West and Congress of Rough Riders of the World at the Columbian Exposition. Uniquely, Cody had been the military scout he played in his show, and he knew both the army generals and the Indians whose real-life experiences undergirded such acts as the attack on the Deadwood Stagecoach and the settler's cabin, the equestrian displays of the rough riders (U.S. cavalry and Indian riders were prominently featured), and the star appearances of such historic figures as Sitting Bull, American Horse, and Short Bull. The program for Buffalo Bill's Wild West carried testimonials to the authenticity of Cody's history and his Wild West; indeed, a broadside declared, "It is not a 'show' in any sense of the word, but it is a series of original, genuine and instructive OBJECT LESSONS in which the participants repeat the heroic parts they have played in actual life upon the plains, in the wilderness, mountain fastness and in the dread and dangerous scenes of savage and cruel warfare." Authenticity—"what really happened"—was what Cody had to sell, and he and Salsbury jealously patrolled the borders of their claim to "the truth."[13]

Like Catlin before him, Buffalo Bill's Wild West gave audiences two views of the *mœurs des sauvages*. A tour of the campground and the domestic arrangements of the Indians and other performers was part of the price of admission, while the acts of the show itself offered a theatrically effective blend of skill and conflict, ending with a unity parade by the entire company. A few blocks north of Buffalo Bill's Wild West, the exposition's Midway Plaisance, managed by the fair's Department of Anthropology, included among its commercial ethnoexhibits an Amerindian village and Sitting Bull's cabin (more than one was advertised at the fair), and show Indians who sought a forum for their side of things, offered a "gash show," or sold goods and forms of entertainment. On the fairground itself a commercial exhibit of parka-clad Inuit, kayaking and managing sled dogs, sweltered through a hot Chicago summer, while the Department of Anthropology offered fairgoers both simulated and actual artifacts from archaeological digs and an "ethnographical village," collecting retrieved and constructed Amerindian dwellings from Canada to Mexico, with Indians of the cultures acting as docents or demonstrating crafts. Nearby, the Bureau of Indian Affairs (BIA) invited fairgoers to an Indian school featuring imported students demonstrating the trade and literacy skills (and Christianity) they were being taught on reservations and at BIA schools across the country. There were also special fair events that featured Indians—parades, dedications, speeches—and fair exhibits, such as a demonstration of Navajo weaving in the Women's Building, that employed them. Inside the Anthropology Building and in that portion of the United States Government Building set aside for the Smithsonian and U.S. Bureau of Ethnology, visitors could see a variety of exhibits testifying to science's take on the authentic.[14]

Buffalo Bill's Wild West and the World's Columbian Exposition of 1893 offer a dizzying array of—sometimes conflicting—performances of "what really happened," of past and present; indeed, the latest news about the last of the Plains Indian wars in Chicago newspapers ran beside updates of fair events. Given the exhibition's theme—the four-hundredth anniversary of Columbus's discovery (as it was then described) of America—collisions between "then" and "now" were as numerous as those between "good" and "evil." The Inuit sued their manager, won, and took over their own management (like the Ojibway in Catlin's day). Simon Pokagon, leader of the Potawatomie, whose ancestors had sold the land where the Columbian Exposition was held to settlers in the early nineteenth century, delivered an impassioned speech against the way those ancestors' descendants were being treated. Rain-in-the-Face appealed for space on the fairgrounds to offer the Indian perspective and was denied (as were black-rights organizations), while the show Indians with Buffalo Bill's Wild West, who had numbered among them Ghost Dancers paroled into Cody's custody, spoke freely to visitors to their campground, as did the English-speaking inhabitants of the Ethnographic Village on the fairground itself. Further uptown, at the newly constructed Art Institute of Chicago, the World Congresses of learned societies gathered, among them the American Historical Association, where Frederick Jackson Turner presented his paper "The Significance of the Frontier in American History." The International Folk-Lore Congress hosted Captain H. L. Scott (Seventh U.S. Cavalry), whose "Sign Language of the Plains Indian" was illustrated by Rain-in-the-Face, Standing Bear, Flat Iron, Painted Horse, and Horse-Comes-Last, performers on the Midway and with Buffalo Bill's Wild West, whose guests the Folk-Lorists were at an afternoon performance on July 12, 1893.[15]

From the midpoint in the story of this conference we can readily look back to the moral moments reflected in Lahontan's, Catlin's, and Cody's performances of the native. Descending to us as the relationship between the perpetuating remembrance and the reminiscence that expresses it, accounts of the other foreground the principles and rules of which the "right conduct" or "customs" of the moral are the reflection. What principles may govern the writing of the ethical in theatre history? None of the stagings I've discussed here would have been considered theatre in its day. All laid claim to the goals of teaching and pleasing. Each remembrance is inseparable from the reminiscence in which it is embedded, yet each claims what it stands for but can never be.

What really happened? What is true, genuine, authentic in Lahontan's Adario, Catlin's Indian Gallery, or Buffalo Bill's Wild West? Are *true, genuine,* or *authentic* words that have any gravity when the subject is theatre or performance? Does the lie come in precisely at the moment when the gap between the story of one and the tales of the many is either ignored (word and deed made the same) or erased (dialectical same as rhetorical same as aesthetic, put another way, fiction made fact, "what really happened" made "the truth")? Scholarship presented at the 2006 Theatre Symposium amply demonstrates the power of the ungenuine, the fictive, the performative to be more true than the true, the point marked by the entry of the moral order, the stuff of *ethnikós*.

The moral order has raised "duty" and "the proper" to new heights in recent years, silencing discussions of racial interaction for fear of offense at the same time that actions in the realm of *ethnikós* have raised the denigration of the Other to new heights, the savage now transferred from North America to Iraq, in a continuation of a colonial discourse wherein the possibility of dialogue has likewise been silenced. The price of the moral order in theatrical research has been and remains very high, while the discourse of *ethikós,* the moral and its practice, incessantly speaks itself in the realm of *ethnikós* in our time, while refusing to think itself, a reminiscence without remembrance on the part of a society that claims "to be what it stands for yet is never able to be." It seems clear to me, in the midst of things, that theatre, which cannot be separated from what it does, has much to teach its culture about ethics and the moral order.

Notes

1. Walter Benjamin, "The Storyteller: Reflections on the Works of Nikolai Leskov," in *Illuminations,* ed. Hannah Arendt, trans. Harry Zohn (New York: Harcourt, Brace and World, 1968), 98; National Public Radio broadcast, March 2006; Theodor Adorno, "Gold Assay," in *Minima Moralia: Reflections from Damaged Life* (Part II: 1945), trans. E. F. N. Jephcott (London: New Left Books, 1974), 155.

2. George Kennedy, *The Art of Persuasion in Greece* (Princeton, NJ: Princeton University Press, 1963), 8.

3. For definitions see the *American College Dictionary* (New York: Random House, 1960), s.v. "ethics."

4. Gordon M. Sayre, *Les sauvages américains: Representations of Native Americans in French and English Colonial Literature* (Chapel Hill: University of North Carolina Press, 1997), 31–34.

5. The third part of Lahontan's book is called *Dialogues curieux entre l'auteur et un sauvage de bon sens qui a voyagé* (in the 1703 English translation, "A Conference or Dialogue between the Author and Adario, a Noted Man among the Savages, containing a Circumstantial View of the Customs and Humours of That People"). See Sayre, *Les sauvages américains,* 37.

6. Hayden White, "The Noble Savage Theme as Fetish," in *First Images of America: The Impact of the New World on the Old,* ed. Fredi Chiapelli (Berkeley: University of California Press, 1976), 1:121. For incessant thought see Michel Foucault, *The Order of Things* (New York: Random House/Vintage Books, 1970). For Adorno see note 1 above.

7. Richard Slotkin and James Folsom, eds., *So Dreadful a Judgment: Puritan Responses to King Philip's War, 1676–1677* (Middletown, CT: Wesleyan University Press, 1978), 231; Sayre, *Les sauvages américains,* 129.

8. The Indian play has been discussed and cataloged in Don B. Wilmeth, "Noble or Ruthless Savage? The American Indian on Stage and in the Drama,"

Journal of American Drama and Theatre 1, no. 1 (spring 1989): 39–73; and Don B. Wilmeth, "Tentative Checklist of Indian Plays (1606–1987)," *Journal of American Drama and Theatre* 1, no. 2 (fall 1989): 34–54. For *Metamora*, specifically, see Jeffrey D. Mason, *Melodrama and the Myth of America* (Bloomington: Indiana University Press, 1993); and the discussions of it and similar works in Rosemarie K. Bank, "Staging the 'Native': Making History in American Theatre Culture, 1828–1838," *Theatre Journal* 45, no. 4 (Dec. 1993): 461–86; Rosemarie K. Bank, *Theatre Culture in America, 1825–1860* (New York: Cambridge University Press, 1997); and Bruce A. McConachie, *Melodramatic Formations: American Theatre and Society, 1820–1870* (Iowa City: University of Iowa Press, 1992).

9. William Truettner's *The Natural Man Observed: A Study of Catlin's Indian Gallery* (Washington, DC: Smithsonian Institution Press, 1979) and Brian W. Dippie's *Catlin and His Contemporaries: The Politics of Patronage* (Lincoln: University of Nebraska Press, 1990) are leading sources for Catlin. For a brief discussion of Catlin's performance work see the epilogue in Bank's *Theatre Culture*. Charles Willson Peale, his museum, and his work and sons are discussed in Charles Coleman Sellers, *Mr. Peale's Museum: Charles Willson Peale and the First Popular Museum of Natural Science and Art* (New York: Norton, 1980)—the peace treaty is discussed on p. 92—and see Sellers's *Charles Willson Peale* (New York: Charles Scribner's Sons, 1969). I discuss the relationship among Peale's, Barnum's, and Kimball's museums in the context of performance in "Archiving Culture: Performance and American Museums in the Early Nineteenth Century," in *Performing America: Cultural Nationalism in American Theater*, ed. Jeffrey D. Mason and J. Ellen Gainor (Ann Arbor: University of Michigan Press, 1999), 37–51.

10. For Catlin's exhibiting, the collation, and his performing see Bank, "Archiving Culture," 43–47. The leader of the second party of Ojibway, Maungwudaus, left a brief account of his travels as a show Indian.

11. A broadside of the acts in Catlin's show at Egyptian Hall in London, 1840–41, is reproduced in Bank, *Theatre Culture*, 179. For museums and the performance of their collections see Susan Vogel, "Always True to the Object, in Our Fashion," in *Exhibiting Cultures: The Poetics and Politics of Museum Display*, ed. Ivan Karp and Steven D. Lavine (Washington, DC: Smithsonian Institution Press, 1991), 191–204; and Barbara Kirshenblatt-Gimblett, *Destination Culture: Tourism, Museums, and Heritage* (Berkeley: University of California Press, 1998). For sightseeing as publicity for Catlin's Indian Gallery see Bank, "Archiving Culture," 45. Catlin discusses playing Indian in London with his white associates and his travels with the Indians in *Catlin's Notes of Eight Years' Travel and Residence in Europe*, 2 vols. (London: n.p., 1848).

12. First among the critics of exhibits of, by, and about Indians is Robert W. Rydell, *All the World's a Fair: Visions of Empire at American International Expositions, 1876–1916* (Chicago: University of Chicago Press, 1984); and see Neil Harris, Wim de Wit, James Gilbert, and Robert W. Rydell, *Grand Illusions: Chicago's World's Fair of 1893* (Chicago: Chicago Historical Society, 1993). Among historians viewing Cody and the Wild West show in a less-transparent

way are L. G. Moses, *Wild West Shows and the Images of American Indians, 1883–1933* (Albuquerque: University of New Mexico Press, 1996); and Joy S. Kasson, *Buffalo Bill's Wild West: Celebrity, Memory, and Popular History* (New York: Hill and Wang, 2000). Though less positive, Richard White's "Frederick Jackson Turner and Buffalo Bill," in *The Frontier in American Culture: An Exhibition at the Newberry Library, August 26, 1994 – January 7, 1995*, ed. James R. Grossman (Berkeley: University of California Press, 1994), 7–65, compares the tropes of the positive and ruthless savage via his title figures and in other sources forming part of the Newberry exhibit.

13. For the Grand Duke Alexis hunting party (General Philip Sheridan and George Armstrong Custer were part of it) see Kasson, *Buffalo Bill's Wild West*, 17; for Buffalo Bill stories and *The Scout of the Prairie* see ibid., 20–27; for the early days of the Wild West show see ibid., 41–63. The broadside is reprinted in Jack Rennert, *100 Posters of Buffalo Bill* (New York: Darien House, 1976), inside back cover.

14. For an account of Buffalo Bill's Wild West and the Columbian Exhibition see Rosemarie K. Bank, "Representing History: Performing the Columbian Exposition," *Theatre Journal* 54, no. 4 (Dec. 2002): 589–606; and Rosemarie K. Bank, "Telling a Spatial History of the Columbian Exposition of 1893," *Modern Drama* 47, no. 3 (fall 2004): 349–66. A gash show involved a performer's gashing (or simulating gashing) his skin.

15. See note 13 for details of and sources for appearances of Indians at the fair and the Congresses (an article by Simon Pokagon also appears in Peyer's anthology, cited in Bank, "Archiving Culture"). Concerning Rain-in-the-Face see Harris et al., *Grand Illusions*, 160. For a facsimile reproduction of Turner's much-studied speech see Turner, *The Significance of the Frontier in American History* (Ann Arbor: University Microfilms, 1966). For Scott and the Lakota see Helen Wheeler Bassett and Frederick Starr, eds., *The International Folk-Lore Congress of the World's Columbian Exposition, Chicago, July 1893* (Chicago: Charles H. Sergel, 1898), 14, 206–20.

What Moral Order?

Observations from the Trenches

Steve Scott

Let me begin with a brief disclaimer. I am from the world of professional theatre, not academics; although I do teach, direct, and occasionally act, I make my living primarily as a producer at the Goodman Theatre in Chicago. To many people, especially certain talent agents I could name, a sentence containing the terms *producer* and *moral order* creates an oxymoron of dizzying proportions. I am also a gay man and (perhaps by self-definition only) an artist, both of which in our current moral and political climate would seem to land me well outside any popularly described definitions of moral norms. Quite frankly, when I was given the topic on which I was expected to speak, I was terrified. What business do I have discussing, especially in the company of scholars much better read in this topic than I, a concept that a majority of people today would say doesn't even include me? What follows, then, is not a researched essay, not a scholarly treatise, but rather my own random thoughts and responses to the topic at hand, based on my own particular vantage point, as well as my discussions with peers, associates, students, and anyone else that I could bully into commenting on the relationship between our art and morality.

When I began thinking about this topic in earnest, I did go to a few of my favorite authors for advice on the question—with some predictably illuminating responses. Lorca, for example, in his 1934 essay "The Authority of the Theatre," offered the following observations:

> The theatre is one of the most useful and expressive instruments for a country's edification, the barometer which registers its greatness or its decline. A theatre that, in every branch, from tragedy to vaudeville, is sensi-

tive and well-oriented, can in a few years change the sensibility of a people, and a broken-down theatre, where wings have given way to cloven hoofs, can coarsen and benumb a whole nation. The theatre is a school of weeping and of laughter, a rostrum where men are free to expose old and equivocal standards of conduct, and explain with living examples the eternal norms of the heart and feelings of man.[1]

I found an even more cogent codification of the various approaches to "moral-based" drama in John Galsworthy's 1909 essay "Some Platitudes Concerning Drama":

> Now, in writing plays, there are, in this matter of the moral, three courses open to the serious dramatist. The first is: To definitely set before the public that which it wishes to have set before it, the views and codes of life by which the public lives and in which it believes. This way is the most common, successful, and popular. It makes the dramatist's position sure, and not too obviously authoritative.
>
> The second course is: To definitely set before the public those views and codes of life by which the dramatist himself lives, those theories in which he himself believes, the more effectively if they are the opposite of what the public wishes to have placed before it, presenting them so that the audience may swallow them like powder in a spoonful of jam.
>
> There is a third course: To set before the public no cut-and-dried codes, but the phenomena of life and character, selected and combined, *but not distorted*, by the dramatist's outlook, set down without fear, favor, or prejudice, leaving the public to draw such poor moral as nature may afford. This third method requires a certain detachment; it requires a sympathy with, a love of, and a curiosity as to, things for their own sake; it requires a far view, together with patient industry, for no immediately practical result.[2]

These are accurate summations, I think, for the theories on which you and I were raised: that one of the primary duties of the theatre artist in society is to question moral authority, moral precepts and pronouncements, in order to refine—or at least shake up—the moral order, the moral status quo.

Armed with these ideas, I then went to a variety of peers and coworkers: fellow staff members at the Goodman Theatre, actors with whom I was working at the time, and my students at the Theatre Conservatory of Roosevelt University, where I'm currently teaching a senior seminar entitled "American Theatre and Social Justice." To all of these groups and individuals I posed what I foolishly thought was a simple question: How do you think the contemporary American theatre comments on, or relates to, the current moral order? The answers I got were unanimous and disturbing: *What* moral order? When I quoted from Lorca or Galsworthy, I was met with stares and in some cases sneers. These writers, I was told, were working in a society in which there existed some real moral order, some sort of prescribed set of moral and social standards that were generally accepted by a majority of people, even if a vocal minority rejected them. But that was then, and this is the twenty-first century, I was told—and in our world that kind of moral order no longer exists. This rather cynical view is best summed up, I think, in Russ Shafer-Landau's study *Whatever Happened to Good and Evil,* which discusses rather eloquently the moral dilemma of the post-9/11 world:

> There is first of all the loss of faith in traditional authority figures. Their edicts once served as moral bedrock for their followers. But we are nowadays far more willing to question the clergy, to doubt their spiritual integrity and to suspect their moral wisdom. And we've scrutinized our secular leaders within an inch of their lives. It hasn't done much to elevate their moral status.
>
> There is also the greater exposure to other cultures, whose practices are incompatible with our own. It is harder to think of one's way of life as the only way, or the only natural way, when so many functioning, intelligent societies are organized along different principles.
>
> Add to this the cautionary tale of our century's fanatics, whose certitude has cost tens of millions their lives. These people were convinced that theirs was the side of Good, that they had a monopoly on the Truth. Wouldn't a little self-doubt have been in order? If we have to choose between the hesitations of those who have their moral doubts, and the fanaticism of those who don't, then perhaps a bit of skepticism isn't such a bad idea after all.
>
> There are also specifically philosophical sources of moral skepticism. If good and evil really exist, then why is there so much disagreement about them? Why isn't there a widely accepted account of how to make moral discoveries? Moreover, if there are correct standards of good and evil, doesn't that license dogmatism and intolerance? Yet if these are the price of good and evil, maybe we do better to abandon such notions. And doesn't the existence of good and evil require the existence of God? But what evidence is there that God exists? Doesn't the amount and degree of sorrow in the world, not to mention the scientific unverifiability of a divine being, give us excellent reason to doubt God's existence?
>
> Taken together, these considerations have done a good deal to convince people to adopt a skeptical attitude toward moral claims. Without an answer to these (and other) worries, too many of us are likely to find ourselves acting and thinking inconsistently. Though firm in our conviction of a terrorist's depravity, we might, in other contexts, find ourselves claim-

ing that our ethical views are merely our opinion, true (if at all) only relative to the culture we live in. . . . The concerns that bring so many of us over [to] the skeptic's side have yet to be dispelled. Until they are, we are likely to be morally schizophrenic: full of outrage at moments, and at other moments just as full of reservations about the status of our moral condemnations.[3]

Interestingly, Shafer-Landau posits that the traumatic events of 9/11 and their aftermath may cause this moral relativism to evolve into a renewed moral objectivity, a clearer set of moral precepts to which a majority of us can subscribe. Unfortunately, this doesn't seem to have happened; instead, the moral polarity that marked the early years of this century seems to have calcified, with each special-interest group (and indeed each individual) clinging almost hysterically to its/his/her particular set of values. In his recent best-seller, *CrazyBusy: Strategies for Coping in a World Gone ADD*, Dr. Edward M. Hallowell translates this moral confusion into practical terms, painting a vivid picture of our moral (and social and political) fragmentation:

> Life today teeters on a pinnacle surrounded by a sea of uncertainty. And so it did well before 9/11 and Hurricane Katrina. . . . But the challenges are peculiar and daunting, more so than most of us realize. For example, how much do you really know about global warming? I didn't know much, [so] I called Jim Anderson, professor of chemistry at Harvard and one of the world's experts on climate. He told me he was not "sanguine" (that's professorese for scared as hell), having looked at the latest data showing how much of the polar ice cap had already melted. As he went into the gory details, the part of my mind that can no longer hear about Big Problems I Can't Solve went numb. And global warming is just *one* of the many challenges we face. AIDS. Resistant bacteria and viruses. Deforestation. A national debt like we've never had before, plus an emerging China holding so many of our notes. The unexplained rise in asthma, autism, allergies, and Asperger's syndrome. Terrorism. . . . From physics to friendships, from cosmology to cameras and computers, from what we do and how others keep track of us, from what your employer can promise you to the lifestyle you can expect, what was familiar has changed. No one knows what will be, what to hold on to, and what to reject.[4]

And nowhere is this confusion-cum-malaise more evident, at least in my informal polling, than with our students. Granted, I grew up in a time when political activism and moral certainty were the hallmarks of our generation, and I have long since seen that fade away. But I expected *some* idealistic fervor, *some* sense of moral righteousness among my students when confronted with my questions about moral codes and moral actions. Instead I got a kind of vehement apathy, an impassioned disavowal from nearly all of my students that a generally agreed-upon moral code could ever, would ever, exist. This is more than an affected world-weary cynicism; these young people were sick to death of the conflicting moral messages that assault them every day, of the quagmire of moral ambiguity that constantly surrounds them. And who could blame them? To them nothing is certain: even that most cherished moral precept, the sanctity of human life, is up for grabs when no one can say for certain when human life begins. And nothing is mysterious or sacrosanct; when every sordid detail of every possible kind of human interaction becomes fodder for your favorite reality show, it's difficult to imagine a moral code that lifts us above these events. Even the concept of morality itself has little impact on them, having become yet another oft-debated plank on the political platform. In a world where both political parties have begun to include moral imperatives as part of their agendas, where every political disagreement seems to inevitably boil down to Good versus Evil, where even the evening news becomes a series of conflicting moral statements (with CNN spouting one moral framework and Fox News another), our students are not just alienated—they're bored, frustrated, and more than a little cynical. And even the most idealistic of them has trouble seeing the theatre as a means of changing this; the words of Lorca and Galsworthy (and Brecht and even Tony Kushner) seem rather quaint to them, interesting perhaps from a historical perspective but rather pointless now, since no one can agree on what needs to be changed in the first place. I should point out that my students are neither privileged slackers nor arrogant intellectuals: they are (largely, anyway) dedicated preprofessionals, most of them with outside jobs to support themselves, and they love their art form—but only for what it does for them, not necessarily for what it does for the world.

So what are we as theatre artists doing about this? How are we responding to this malaise? Not well, if you listen to a few of our more outspoken peers. Recently in a *New York Times* interview, British playwright David Hare used the occasion of the opening of his play *Stuff Happens* to offer a rather mordant view of American theatre in the twenty-first century: "Certainly from Los Angeles my impression is that the American audience is way ahead of the American theater establishment," Mr. Hare said, speaking of the 2005 production. "For some reason in America the theater has also been largely collusive in offering escapist entertainment, as if we were living through the Depression or as if we were living through a war that we all agree on. Actually, we're fighting a war that we don't agree on. And I wish I saw more signs in the American theater of that dissent being dramatized."[5]

Although Hare's point of view is specifically political, it's difficult not to agree with him when perusing the New York theatre listings for the week just past. The most serious examination of American moral values can be found not in a new play by a young firebrand author but in a revival of Odets's Depression-era classic *Awake and Sing*. And the most popular commercial hits of the day either reduce the issue of moral values to a kind of retro morality that seems to echo values from a half-century ago *(Wicked)* or flaunt those values altogether *(The Producers)*. Even the stage version of *Hairspray* downplays the rather muted plea for racial tolerance that characterized the film on which it was based in favor of outrageous costumes and frenetic dancing. Obviously, the Broadway musical has never been the most trenchant critic of moral values, but it's been a long road from the passionate (if somewhat romantic) social morality of *South Pacific* to *Spamalot*. And in the noncommercial theatre, both in New York and elsewhere, the tyranny of political correctness further erodes many attempts to deal seriously with contemporary issues of morality and society; the recent flap surrounding the New York Theatre Workshop's postponement of *My Name Is Rachel Corrie* is in part the result of a tendency to brand legitimate social questioning as "racist," "fascist," or simply inappropriate. The result? More artistic work that avoids moral questioning or does pose moral questions only in terms of the artist's personal morality. The discussion becomes one about "my code" and "your code," not a moral code that we can all debate and to which we can all subscribe.

As to Hare's assertion that the American audience is "way ahead" of the American theatre establishment—well, maybe. Interestingly, the audience response to two recent productions at the Goodman Theatre indicates to me that our audiences are as morally confused as our artists. Last season, for example, we produced Doug Wright's *I Am My Own Wife*, a powerful study of a German transvestite who survived both Nazism and communism through a variety of means, not all of them admirable. Interestingly, our audiences (most of whom loved the show) picked up on neither the moral ambiguities of the central character's actions nor the less-decorous descriptions of sexual acts and ideas; at every postperformance discussion their responses centered solely on the "heroism" of the central character, the "inspiration" of the triumph against adversity that the play celebrates. (The play does do that but in much less certain terms than our audiences saw.) A few months later we produced Rebecca Gilman's new adaptation of Ibsen's *Dollhouse*, a contemporary version of the play in which Nora decides *not* to leave at the end of the play but stays to live out (probably) a grimly compromised marriage. Although this ending was truer to the contemporary setting of the adaptation (and, arguably, to Ibsen's original intent), our audiences hated it because it robbed Nora of a kind of heroism that they found compelling. Never mind that in Ibsen's original Nora's leaving was more a form of social suicide than the establishment of a heroic world order; the Goodman audiences, sophisticated and intelligent as they are, still needed that heroic optimism to make the play mean something to them. Susan Sontag commented on this perhaps peculiarly American trait in a 1995 interview:

> Well, Americans are very devoted to the idea of hope, aren't we? This is a society built on the notion of the new life, the second chance, start all over again, be reborn, you can always change yourself, if you want it to be so you can make it so—all those ideas of improvement and self-remaking, which usually involve breaking away from one's own individual history or past, or some collective history or identity such as the country or culture you came from.
>
> And there is—well, there was—a very strong idea of justice in this country. But I think most of our ideas about justice and righteous action involved shunting to the side a sense of how large the capacity for wickedness in human beings is.[6]

Ultimately, it may be this drive for hope that's fragmenting us most now. Lacking comfort in societal codes, confused by the lack of generally accepted norms, bombarded by news reports in which even the colors red and blue have taken on a kind of simplistic moral symbolism, we (students, artists, and audiences) look for reassurance in a nostalgic moral code that may have been true fifty years ago, or by retreating into ourselves, our computers and iPods, our online games where we can decimate whole cultures with the flick of a finger.

Do I exaggerate? Possibly. But the fact is that the concept of "moral order" is a tricky one just now and one that doesn't seem to make sense to a lot of people, including our own young artists. Can the theatre help to restore a sense of order, a sense of collectiveness, of community, of the things that do indeed tie us together rather than separate us? These are the questions that I hope we can ponder in the next few days as we examine a number of particular topics, some concerning similar struggles in the past and others dealing with more contemporary issues. And as we do that, I'd like us to keep the following words in mind, the words of Arthur Miller from his 1967 essay "The Contemporary Theater":

> You have to ask yourself fundamental questions as to why there should be a theater. Maybe there shouldn't be. Maybe it's a dead art. Maybe it ought to be dead. Maybe what we want is a sculpture of the automobile, which sometimes isn't bad, and the jazz that we have, which is sometimes wonderful, and the popular arts that we really take to, that take no efforts on our parts to enjoy. I always dislike the idea of people having to go to these damned things, to the theater. It's like people wanting to be better. They shouldn't want to be better; they should need this thing the way they need food. And I'm not sure we do. Maybe there's something farcical and unreal about it all that we're trying to prop up with new buildings.
>
> Well, that ought to depress you enough. I would only add a most important thing, which is that it can't die. It can't die because we must have, in order to live at all, some kind of symbolization of our lives. The theater is not like life. Life is like the theater. We have to have, whether it be in some deserted basement or in a great building, an art which expresses, more fully than any individual can, the collective consciousness of people, what they share with each other, and where they're different. So that we can become individuals again we have to become a spiritual unity again. That's what it can do, and the need for it will always be there. So I'm not ultimately pessimistic but simply trying to warn us all that we have not got the solution now, but it's worth thought if one cares about it at all.[7]

Thank you for listening to my ramblings this evening; I'm looking forward to your presentations this weekend.

Notes

1. Federico Garcia Lorca, "The Authority of the Theatre," in *Playwrights on Playwriting,* ed. Toby Cole (New York: Hill and Wang, 1961), 45.

2. John Galsworthy, "Some Platitudes Concerning Drama," in *Playwrights on Playwriting,* ed. Toby Cole (New York: Hill and Wang, 1961), 45–46.

3. Russ Shafer-Landau, *Whatever Happened to Good and Evil?* (New York: Oxford University Press, 2004), 4–5.

4. Edward M. Hallowell, *CrazyBusy: Overstretched, Overbooked, and About to Snap! Strategies for Coping in a World Gone ADD* (New York: Ballantine, 2006), 16–17.

5. "David Hare Enters the Theater of War," *New York Times,* March 26, 2006, Arts and Leisure sec., 16.

6. Susan Sontag, "On Art and Politics," in *Tony Kushner in Conversation*, ed. Robert Vorlicky (Ann Arbor: University of Michigan Press, 1998), 172–73.

7. Arthur Miller, "The Contemporary Theater," in *The Theater Essays of Arthur Miller,* ed. Robert A. Martin and Steven R. Centola (New York: Da Capo, 1996), 308.

William Dunlap, Father of American Theatre—and American Antitheatricality

David Carlyon

CONSIDERATION OF antitheatricality inevitably points at those who would censor theatre, diminish it, control it, or shut it down. Jonas Barish's book *The Antitheatrical Prejudice* powerfully conveys the battle between outside pressure and hardy defense.[1] Even for those who have not read the book, its title has become a byword for prejudice against our field. We, the People of the Theatre, it says, are besieged, sometimes laughably, sometimes dangerously, by antitheatricality. That sense of oppression figures heavily in accounts of the career of William Dunlap (1766–1839), "Father of the American Theatre." (Current practice usually puts that grandiloquent phrase in quotation marks to acknowledge past usage and to indicate scholarly discomfort with the thorny nature of such usage.) As Barish points out, however, antitheatricality rumbles inside theatre as well. He argues that it is a fundamental human trait and that the urge of theatricality is matched by equally strong suspicion of theatricality. As Barish titles his last chapter, it's "Theater Against Itself." Though American theatre has focused its energy on fighting external foes, the internalized suspicion of theatricality remains. That manifestly applies to Dunlap. Though he deserves honor for his pioneering role, he also pioneered a strong ambivalence in and about theatre. He did not create American antitheatricality any more than he created American theatricality, yet his influential writing exhibits his distaste for actors, distrust of audiences, and appeals for censorship. Those hesitations about dramatic representation reveal in this model and source for what would follow the antitheatricality deep within the heart of American theatricality.[2]

Dunlap's many early contributions to the field led to the label "Father of American Theatre." He was the country's first professional manager, a nonactor running the John Street Theatre, and then Park Theatre, with the actors Lewis Hallam Jr. and John Hodgkinson (1796–97), with Hodgkinson (1797–98), then on his own (1798–1805), and finally for Thomas Abthorpe Cooper (1806–11). He was the United States' first professional playwright, author of more than fifty translations and plays, the most well-known of which is *André*, the 1797 play usually mentioned in accounts of Dunlap. He was its first historian, author of *A History of the American Theatre* in 1832, giving him pride of place in the field of American theatre history; one might say he was the first Americanist. Finally, in 1837 he wrote one of the first American novels using theatre as its setting, *Thirty Years Ago; or, The Memoirs of a Water Drinker*. (Remarkably Dunlap probably had greater prominence as a pioneer in American fine arts, as a painter who studied in London with Benjamin West and painted George Washington, made his living as an itinerant creating miniature portraits, led the American Academy of Fine Arts, and helped found the National Academy of Design, as well as writing a seminal work in *this* field, the 1834 *History of the Rise and Progress of the Arts of Design in the United States*. Theatre students may know this aspect of Dunlap without realizing it, through his frequently reprinted frontispiece image from *The Contrast*.)[3]

Dunlap's life and times certainly fit the familiar notion of Theatre Besieged. His *History* recorded examples we still employ. In 1774 the Continental Congress, discouraging theatre, offered the insult of lumping it with gambling and cockfighting. The Puritans of Massachusetts banned theatre in 1750 after a crowd's eagerness to see a show at a coffeehouse led to a public disturbance; the ban was not lifted until 1793, and even at that late date it required a protracted fight. The many instances cataloged in Dunlap's book continue to show what the philistines have done and, by inference, what they are doing or might do. Here is the antitheatrical prejudice in blatant and cautionary array.[4]

Dunlap's own career reinforced that message of antitheatrical prejudice from forces outside theatre, as his endeavor to make plays a force for social good constantly butted against pressure and unsympathetic audiences. He went bankrupt as a manager, struggling to reconcile his tastes with the tastes of his audiences. His dramatic writing made little money, and *André*, "one of the best plays of the early American stage," had only three performances before he had to alter it into a sporadically produced patriotic piece, *The Glory of Columbia—Her Yeomanry!* Dunlap knew well the dissipation that its foes used as ammunition against theatre. He went broke managing the Park Theatre partly because the drinking of Hallam's actress-wife, Miss Tuke, caused discord in the company. When George Frederick Cooke arrived for the 1810-11 season, Dunlap had another personal encounter with drunkenness as he was engaged to travel with this first English star to tour the United States, less as a companion than as a chaperone to try to keep Cooke sober enough to perform.[5] Finally, in the standard story, bowed down but not beaten, Dunlap looked back over his career to convey his disappointments and theatre's weaknesses as he wrote his *History of American Theatre*, which helped create the field that would later honor him as "Father." Carrying the theme of disappointed struggle through to the end of Dunlap's career, even that seminal *History* did not sell well.[6]

His personal life reinforces the image of struggle, for his brother-in-law was Timothy Dwight, noted preacher, president of Yale University, and fierce opponent of things theatrical. Dwight bundled his biases into his "Essay on the Stage," published posthumously in 1824. So pronounced was his opposition that Barish used him as a prime example of antitheatrical prejudice: theatrical activity following the Revolutionary War "retreated into the universities, where even so it could fall under the lash of precisians like Timothy Dwight, who warned his students at Yale that to frequent the theater was to lose their souls." Perhaps worse, Dwight described a hypothetical person who presumed to disagree with him as a "superficial thinker." This was (remains?) a potent attack because it struck at a fundamental insecurity of theatre people, that their work is lesser intellectually, that they are in effect sitting at the children's table of play while other public thinkers—poets, philosophers, preachers, writers—are engaged in more profound, deeper, more *adult* issues. That attack at least appears to have stung Dunlap. His public memoirs refer to the intellectual pleasures of evenings with Dwight, but his private diaries relate their disagreements. Imagine how awkward family gatherings must have been: "Hello, Timothy. How are your roses?" "Fine, William. Are you still promoting the rank degradation of superficial players and the eternal damnation of the benighted masses by fostering the unspeakable work of Satan?"[7]

Dunlap framed his career as a struggle, and historians have followed suit, offering a stirring narrative of battle against artistic compromises imposed by commercial considerations and against those who would degrade theatre. In the introduction to their collection *American Drama: Colonial to Contemporary*, Stephen Watt and Gary A. Richardson suggested that Dunlap's life was "particularly illustrative of the difficulties" facing early playwrights. Richardson was more specific in an earlier book, writing that Dunlap sought financial success by producing work he considered less worthy, overcoming his own reservations about such plays, which Richardson described as "designed to discourage, if not prevent, audience reflection." According to David Grimsted, Dunlap "often sullied his ideals" in his struggles to present audiences with profound theatrical fare. Introducing the modern reprint of Dunlap's *History of the American Theatre,* Tice L. Miller depicted as a poignancy that Dunlap "realized he had lowered his personal standards to gain an audience." Miller goes on to express the cri de coeur of theatre practitioners from that era to our own: Dunlap faltered despite his courageous attempts "to uplift the American stage."[8]

To repeat Barish's insight, however, "antitheatrical prejudice" is more than the convenient dichotomy of theatre against its foes. Just as Barish intended more than a diatribe against theatre's enemies, the neat picture of Dunlap struggling against antitheatrical forces is incomplete. His struggles included a powerful ambivalence.

That ambivalence is palpable from the first pages of his *History*. Paired epigraphs set the defensive tone: "Where's that palace where into sometimes / Foul things intrude not?" and "The corruption of the theatre is no disproof of its innate and primitive utility." His preface begins literally with an apology, quoting Colley Cibber's *Apology* that the increase of London playhouses meant that the stage was "of course reduced . . . to live upon the gratification of such hearers as they knew would be best pleased with public offense." Dunlap's own words did not improve the view, as he depicted playwrights and actors being out of control: the "course of progressive civilization" had freed poets and players from the need for a patron's protection; but "like other slaves, at the moment of acquiring liberty, they were inclined to become licentious." More than simply inclining toward sin, theatre "became mischievous as the encourager of licentiousness." What had become popular was "every deviation from 'plain sense and nature.'" These first few pages offer nearly nothing about the glories of theatre or any benefits to society. The first chapter's first section, "Use and Abuse of Theatre," continues the ambivalence. Even as Dunlap presents his main argument, that drama and "the state of manners" in a country rise together, he leaps to more apology: "That there are evils, and perversions, and abuses attendant upon theatrical exhibitions, . . . no one is more ready to admit than the writer." A political candidate admitting as much might as well cede the election. Ostensibly combating prejudice, Dunlap adds his own examples instead, and disparagement continues throughout the history. He pleads for the better sort to remain loyal because "[i]f the theatre is abandoned to the uneducated, the idle, and the profligate, mercenary managers will please their visitors by such ribaldry or folly, or worse, as is attractive to such patrons." As the dire but inevitable consequence, theatre "will attract the idle and the vicious by such entertainments as suits their ignorance or depravity." So go Dunlap's defensive attacks through to the concluding chapter. He applauds Mrs. Trollope, the British traveler whose sharp criticisms of the United States earned his countrymen's enmity. He deplores the "deterioration of the drama" and complains that the improvement in acting pushed quality writers into closet dramas, afraid that their polished words would be degraded by histrionic skill. Dunlap characterizes theatre as a necessary evil, deciding that the elite may have achieved a level of refinement that made the elevating effects of theatre unnecessary but arguing the "mass of mankind" still required its ministrations. He sought to define theatricality virtually out of existence by declaring that the theatre of America means the *drama* of America, that is, its literary efforts. For emphasis—what one might otherwise label "dramatic emphasis"—he repeats his epigraph that there is no "palace whereinto sometimes foul things intrude not." Once again insisting that the ideal is an institution "supported and guided by the state," he dreams aloud of his "theatrical millennium," when "plays are not submitted to the decision of the ignorant"—that is, audiences. From beginning to end antitheatricality permeates Dunlap's seminal account of American theatre.[9]

Dunlap did not isolate this prejudice in his *History*, an insider's caution to fellow insiders. He made it even more starkly clear in the novel he wrote five years later, *Thirty Years Ago; or, The Memoirs of a Water Drinker*.[10] Expanding on the theme introduced in his *History* of theatre's dissipation, he based his new book on his experience of touring with Cooke and his struggles to keep the English star sober. Usually described as a temperance novel, *Memoirs of a Water Drinker* does depict the evils of alcohol but equally displays what Dunlap considered the evils of theatre. So pronounced is the book's bias against the stage that if one did not know his background, one might easily infer that the author had been a particularly virulent foe of theatre, worse in his comprehensive condemnations than that "precisian" Dwight.

The book's hero, Zebediah Spiffard, is a comic actor known to his friends as "Spif." As the titular "water drinker," that is, one who has chosen to drink water rather than liquor, the era's other common beverage, he must deal with two drunken colleagues. One is an English star, clearly modeled on Cooke. The other is his actress wife, based on Hallam's wife, whose drinking caused the backstage discord at the Park Theatre that propelled Dunlap's bankruptcy. That unpleasantness clearly remained a sore point with Dunlap three decades after the fact. At first our hero, Spif, doesn't know about his wife's drinking. But when his fellow actors trick him into thinking he must fight a duel—a fictional version of a prank played on Thomas Abthorpe Cooper[11]—his nervousness makes him preoccupied, prompting her to fear that he has discovered her drinking, which pushes her to drink more. The downward spiral continues until—faithful to temperance tale tropes—she dies. As a consequence Spif quits the theatre, becomes a preacher, and moves to the South. (The change in setting provided Dunlap a platform on which to indulge two other favorite topics of the era's reformers, slavery and Southern indolence.)

Though it may seem inevitable that its reputed father would employ theatre to provide the background for his novel, Dunlap spent his life in a variety of pursuits that would have served equally well. He was a merchant, following his wealthy father, making a mercantile setting a possibility.[12] He was a man of letters with friendships among the young nation's literary elite, including William Cullen Bryant and James Fenimore Cooper, to whom he dedicated his theatre *History,* so he could have placed his novel in a literary salon. In the art world, where his history of that field gave him a continuing prominence greater than in theatre, he could have used his study in London for an exotic locale; his encounter with George Washington as he painted his portrait could have prompted a Revolutionary War novel, just as his look at his country's past prompted a Revolutionary War play, *André;* his experience as an itinerant would have provided a wide geographical scope; and his work with a fine arts academy and an academy of design must have given him familiarity in institutional infighting. That latter experience, added to what he knew of his brother-in-law's life at Yale, might have inspired him to write the first American satire of university life. Yet ignoring all other possible situations his diverse background had showered on him, he chose to set his novel in the world of theatre, to continue his argument that theatre encourages vice.

For theatre is not simply a backdrop to Dunlap's temperance sermon. It is a coextensive evil. He describes Spif's original look backstage:

> What he there saw at first disgusted him . . . beauty [changed] to deformity. That which had pleased the eye as the glow of health, was, in reality, a coarse white and red daubing, associated in his mind, from infancy, with disease or moral depravity. The modest mien assumed before the audience, was sometimes suddenly dismissed, after passing the side scene, and replaced by coarse mirth, or coarser rage. The devout or patient hero would instantly be converted into a fury, venting curses upon the prompter or call-boy. . . . [A]ll the order, harmony, and splendour of

the scenes [was transformed] into confusion, wrangling, the darkness of smoking lamps, and the jostling of dirty scene-shifters and vulgar supernumeraries.[13]

The Father of American Theatre was notably unfond of his progeny.

Other instances of antitheatricality abound in Dunlap's novel, such as his description of the situation of Spif's wife. Mrs. Spiffard was

> one of the acknowledged heroines of the stage at this time, but as utterly shut out from female society as if she had been infected with the most deadly contamination. . . . It is in vain to deny, or endeavor to conceal from the actress, that the very circumstances of publicly exhibiting for hire, that person, and those talents, so admired and applauded, has degraded her in the eyes of the world.

It might be tempting to see protofeminism here except that Dunlap approved this state of affairs. Immediately following this litany of theatrical female woe, he editorialized: "Be it just or unjust, *so it is;* and perhaps, so it ought to be." In another key episode, when a young relative of Spif's is molested, she demands of her attacker, "What have you seen in me that could induce you to persecute me?" The villain retorts blithely and—in the fictional world Dunlap has established—justifiably, "Your visits to the private door of the theatre." Her mere presence backstage makes her fair game for molestation. The molester starts to elaborate on his explanation but suavely refrains out of a delicate sense of duty to polite society: "I saw you with—and apparently dependent upon people whose profession—and as the world says—but I will not offend." He would accost her, force himself on her, rape her, but he is too much the gentleman to offend by speaking aloud the evil of theatre. (Rosemarie K. Bank's cogent point about Dunlap's *History*, that his depiction of degraded theatre localized anxiety on the female body, has particular force here.)[14]

Dunlap's harsh judgment on theatre as revealed in the novel culminates in his hero's departure from the profession. Though prompted by sadness at his wife's death, Spif quits for a grander reason, his disgust at the degradations of his erstwhile profession. He ceases all association with theatre, and Dunlap highlights for his readers the stirring reason why: "Society has raised a bar between the preacher and the player."[15]

What lay behind this pronounced disdain for theatre? Heather Nathans attributes early American antitheatricality to the struggle to break cultural ties to England. But Dunlap had more in mind than that distant kingdom. His suspicion of the stage blended with suspicion of the democratic forces permeating the young republic. S. E. Wilmer has examined the partisanship in Dunlap's plays, noting especially that *André* "was implicitly questioning . . . egalitarian values and reinforcing notions of social hierarchy." Dunlap may have disagreed about theatre attendance with his brother-in-law, Timothy Dwight, but they were of one mind in their dread of vox populi. They both worried that the still-new experiment in governance might go, or had already gone, too far. Dunlap departed a Methodist church service because of that growing sect's then-notorious roof-raising enthusiasm. The biographer Robert Canary points out that Dunlap, writing to James Fenimore Cooper, blamed street riots on immigrants and in an address to art students declared that the "uninstructed laborer in civilized society is nearly as dead to those objects which fill us with delight, as the savage." It should be noted that Dunlap wrote his antitheatrical-infused works, *History of Theatre* and *Thirty Years Ago; or, The Memoirs of a Water Drinker,* three decades after his own career in theatre but in the middle of the Jacksonian era, when audiences were asserting themselves more and the "better sort" had become apprehensive of the participatory turn America was taking. Theatre historians have depicted Dunlap's departure from theatre as a necessary but graceful retirement from a field that had given him little but heartache. A literary scholar may have come closer to the mark, however, writing of Dunlap's "retreat from theater to the safer, more elite precincts of fine art." Because Dunlap records in his diary that he never contradicted his brother-in-law, Dwight, publicly, Grimsted interpreted that as an example of politeness, the "circumspection and tolerance" of the well-bred. Just as likely, Dunlap fundamentally agreed with Dwight. Bluntly, both men believed people must be controlled. Dwight urged it in church, college, and politics; Dunlap sought it in theatre.[16]

Even Dunlap's advocacy of government support for theatre, which would seem praiseworthy in later eras, stemmed from this overarching bias. With a grand "Plan of and Wish for Reform," he urged public funding to achieve government control of the stage, the better to prevent "the evils flowing from theatrical representation." He envisioned how to accomplish his cherished ideal, "an association of men of taste, literature, and moral standing [to make theatre] a school that shall invite to virtue." This elite would seek out and employ actors "selected for their morals as well as talents." Dunlap worried that theatre otherwise would be like rogues on holiday "throwing . . . [fire]crackers at all spectators without distinction." And he was keen on making distinctions. His ideal leaders, this "powerful association of men . . . of refinement, taste, and experience in the fine arts," would include no actors. After all, he was America's first manager who was not himself an actor. This dismissive attitude was not simply public posturing. Like a character in a melodrama, he ensured in his own life that no player darkened his door, for as Grimsted notes, he "made a point of going out to visit his theatrical associates rather than inviting them to his home." He believed actors were extravagant creatures who inevitably fell into excess trying to please audiences. Dunlap objected to Boston's half-century ban on theatre but also objected to the performers violating the ban: "Thus were the laws defied, and the people and their magistrates insulted." As summarized in the concluding chapter of his *History*, he acknowledged that American acting had been improving, but the playwright in him thought that improvement "injurious to the drama" and that the actors' talent overwhelmed "the author's images," pushing the skilled writer away from theatre. In his novel Dunlap depicted his actor hero as too honest to "wear the mask" in life, a nod to personal sincerity that nonetheless carries a whiff of suspicion of acting.[17] Not surprisingly, Dunlap also distrusted audiences. He asserted that they preferred degraded entertainments unless guided by their betters. One of the degradations he cited in his *History* was the large size of the new playhouses, which he argued led managers to pander to base tastes to fill them. Combating that would be his proposed elite of New York literary men who, he fantasized, would form "themselves into a species of dramatic censorship."[18]

Dunlap's blatant antitheatricality does not contradict the fact that he did face genuine opposition or that abuses roiled the theatre of his day. He went broke trying to find plays that appealed both to audiences and to his sense of moral and instructive fare. Riots plagued the playhouses, and religion kept battering at their doors.[19] Sympathy for his struggles, however, should not obviate the historian's need to see more clearly that in this country, theatre history, and in significant ways, theatre itself, was fostered in suspicion of the theatrical impulse. As Jonas Barish suggests and as William Dunlap demonstrated with his apologies and arguments for control, the antitheatrical prejudice works within theatre too. The Father of American Theatre was also Father of American Antitheatricality.

It would be convenient to ignore the rampant antitheatricality in Dunlap's career, excusing him as a forefather with a fetish, except that his influence and example sounded down the years. As Grimsted has pointed out, Dunlap "did much to advance ideas that were to become preeminent in the nineteenth century."[20] For all his genuine struggles, the influential ideas he advanced include continuing suspicion of the theatrical urge. For instance, the vibrant theatricality of nineteenth-century audiences engaging the stage got shrunk into the Rube Story, my label for the plethora of urban legends of hicks talking back to actors because they were supposedly too stupid to know they were at a play. These fictions continue to be repeated in our histories as fact at least in part because the fictive image of ignorantly excessive rubes in the seats reinforces the underlying notion of primitive excess on the early American stage, a notion accepted as fact more often than examined.[21] Word usage offers another example, as *melodramatic* shifted from description into sneer as self-proclaimed reformers decided that American theatre had been negligible until O'Neill and that standards rose highest in theatre that was quietest. Contrast the English stage tradition of veneration for its great actors of generations past with the American habit of dismissing past greatness, assuming, for instance, that Edwin Forrest must have been a bombastic ranter and, thanks to the sniping of his playwright-son Eugene, that James O'Neill was a talent-wasting hack. (That filial sneer echoed Dunlap's depiction of Cooke as a great talent wasted.) Meanwhile historians, taking sides, repeated polemics as facts. Richardson posits that Dunlap's problems stemmed from producing plays "designed to discourage, if not prevent, audience reflection," a faux-echt Brechtian notion that theatre is best when it is pedagogy.[22] Even as modern theorists insist that the idea of progress is a hegemonic relic of the Victorian ideal of moral improvement, the notion persists as an article of faith that American theatre has progressed beyond its coarse pioneers. It may be a congenial faith, for it flatters contemporary theatre, but it is faith nonetheless rather than carefully examined analysis.

Not that antitheatricality within theatre is all bad. Yeats declared that fights with others generate rhetoric, while fights with ourselves yield poetry. It may be that the best work in theatre emerges not from conscious, determined attempts to challenge or enlighten others but from struggles to reconcile inner conflict. That struggle generally, and perhaps its manifestation in the ongoing conflict between theatricality and antitheatricality, may be when theatre most genuinely challenges or enlightens—and excites.

None of this is to deny the threats and attacks theatre has to face. One need not be paranoid to notice that the moralist mob thrives in every generation, not to mention its concomitant urge to control dramatic enactments that displease. Similarly audiences pop up in every age to scorn any stage work except the easiest, broadest, emptiest. Nevertheless, despite dangerous attacks and dull crowds, American theatre has had wiggle room, chances to do in the live moment of the stage what might otherwise be restrained or restricted. Yet in that relative freedom, from Dunlap's day on, it has veered away from a fervent embrace of the theatricality that is as much our birthright as nervousness about it. So it is incumbent on historians to be aware of this innate battle in theatre, if we are to approach a narrative conveying the living complexity of the past. In our time as in Dunlap's, it's not us against them. It's us against us.

Notes

1. Jonas Barish, *The Antitheatrical Prejudice* (Berkeley: University of California Press, 1981).

2. Ibid. Barish's examples of the theatre's ambivalence include discussion of Ben Jonson (132–54), examination of the nineteenth century (295–349), and his final chapter (450–77).

3. David Grimsted, *Melodrama Unveiled: American Theater and Culture, 1800–1850* (Berkeley: University of California Press, 1987), esp. 1–9, 15–23; Tice L. Miller's introduction to William Dunlap, *A History of the American Theatre from Its Origins to 1832* (Urbana: University of Illinois Press, 2005); Robert H. Canary, *William Dunlap* (New York: Twayne, 1970). Dunlap's frontispiece can be seen in Barry B. Witham, ed., *Theatre in the United States: A Documentary History*, vol. 1, *1750–1915: Theatre in the Colonies and United States* (Cambridge, UK: Cambridge University Press, 1996), 34.

4. See, e.g., Dunlap, *History*, 39, 67–68, 128–33.

5. Peter A. Davis, "Plays and Playwrights to 1800," in *The Cambridge History of American Theatre*, vol. 1, *Beginnings to 1870*, ed. Don B. Wilmeth and Christopher Bigsby (Cambridge, UK: Cambridge University Press, 1998), 245; S. E. Wilmer, "Partisan Theatre in the Early Years of the United States," *Theatre Survey* 40, no. 2 (Nov. 1999): 13–14; Don B. Wilmeth, "Cooke among the Yankee Doodles," *Theatre Survey* 14, no. 2 (Nov. 1973): 1–32; Don B. Wilmeth, *George Frederick Cooke: Machiavel of the Stage* (Westport, CT: Greenwood Press, 1980).

6. Nor has Dunlap's *History* always pleased his professional successors. George O. Seilhamer, in his own *History of the American Theatre: During the Revolution and After*, 2 vols. (Philadelphia: Globe, 1889), gave the back of his hand to his illustrious predecessor. Dunlap's "statements of fact are almost always misstatements," meaning that "the stream of American theatrical history was poisoned at its source." Ultimately, "[s]o many and so inexcusable were Dunlap's inaccuracies that it is impossible not to wonder at the mental equipment of a man who could be guilty of them." Seilhamer was equally harsh about Dunlap's other careers. His paintings were "wretched caricatures," his frontispiece to *The Contrast* "would have been discreditable to a self-taught amateur," he failed as a manager "through his want of knowledge of the the-

atrical business," his *Water Drinker* was only a "so-called novel," and his other books showed him to be a "hack writer" (Seilhamer, *History*, 2:273-76). Seilhamer did not disparage Dunlap's gardening skills.

7. On "precisians" see Barish, *Antitheatrical Prejudice*, 296, quoting Léonie Villard, *Le théâtre américain* (Paris: Bolvin, 1929); on "superficial" see Grimsted, *Melodrama Unveiled*, 6; Canary, *William Dunlap*, 20.

8. Stephen Watt and Gary A. Richardson, *American Drama: Colonial to Contemporary* (Fort Worth, TX: Harcourt Brace College, 1995), 12; Gary A. Richardson, *American Drama from the Colonial Period through World War I* (New York: Twayne, 1993), 54; Grimsted, *Melodrama Unveiled*, 18; Miller, introduction, xvii-xviii. Van Wyck Brooks offers an earlier version of this perspective in "William Dunlap and His Circle," in *The World of Washington Irving* (New York: Dutton, 1944), 152-75.

9. Dunlap, *History*, 1-3, 5, 72-73, 403-6. A psychological perspective on Dunlap's ambivalence can be found in Lucy Rinehart, "'Manly Exercises': Post-Revolutionary Performances of Authority in the Theatrical Career of William Dunlap," *Early American Literature* 36, no. 2 (Sep. 2001): 263-94.

10. William Dunlap, *Thirty Years Ago; or, The Memoirs of a Water Drinker*, 2 vols. (New York, 1837).

11. Ibid., 1:121.

12. The guardian angel who leads Spif from the degradations of theatre is a merchant, the "beloved ... and trusted" James Littlejohn, a "good man" (ibid., 1:129-31).

13. Ibid., 1:78-79.

14. Ibid., 1:166; 2:87; Rosemarie K. Bank, *Theatre Culture in America, 1825-1860* (Cambridge, UK: Cambridge University Press, 1997), 128-30.

15. Dunlap, *Water Drinker*, 2:130.

16. Heather S. Nathans, *Early American Theatre from the Revolution to Thomas Jefferson: Into the Hands of the People* (Cambridge, UK: Cambridge University Press, 2003), 6; Wilmer, "Partisan Theatre," 13; Grimsted, *Melodrama Unveiled*, 4; Canary, *William Dunlap*, 37, 45-46; Grimsted, *Melodrama Unveiled*, 6. On Dunlap's possible "retreat" see Rinehart, "'Manly Exercises,'" 14.

17. Dunlap, *Water Drinker*, 1:187, also 1:183-84.

18. Ibid., 363-65, 72, 2, 356; Grimsted, *Melodrama Unveiled*, 2; Dunlap, *History*, 131-33, 216, 197.

19. Richard Butsch, "American Theater Riots and Class Relations, 1754-1849," *Theatre Annual* 43 (1995): 41-59; Claudia D. Johnson, "The Theatre's Qualified Victory in an Old War," *Theatre Survey* 25, no. 2 (Nov. 1984): 193-210.

20. Grimsted, *Melodrama Unveiled*, 1.

21. David Carlyon, "'blow your nose with your fingers': The Rube Story as Crowd Control," *New England Theatre Journal* 7 (1996): 1-22.

22. Richardson, *American Drama*, 54.

"NOT from the Drowsy Pulpit!"

The Moral Reform Melodrama on the Nineteenth-Century Stage

John W. Frick

IN A FEBRUARY 1871 ARTICLE in the *Galaxy* magazine the novelist and legendary storyteller Mark Twain made a claim that to the casual observer of today's theatre—especially of Broadway—might seem preposterous: namely, that nine-tenths of the American populace learned their morals *not* from the "drowsy pulpits" of the country's churches but from the stages of its theatres.[1] While it is conceivable that Twain was simply referencing in general the dominant form of nineteenth-century drama—melodrama—regarded by Peter Brooks, David Grimsted, Bruce McConachie, Rosemarie Bank, Elaine Hadley, and other experts on the subject as the era's morality play, it is equally likely that he had in mind a particularly polemic and didactic subtype of melodrama: the moral reform drama.[2] This essay will examine various aspects of this often overlooked subgenre—the ways in which the moral reform drama differed from other forms of melodrama; its influence on the dominant ideology of the era; its role in expanding and changing the gender and class composition of the antebellum theatre audience; and its serving as a harbinger of a more socially conscious drama to follow in the nineteenth century and early in the twentieth—plays like *The City*, by Clyde Fitch, and Ned Sheldon's *Salvation Nell*.

In his seminal study of melodrama Bruce McConachie has distinguished between the various strains of the form and has codified a typology that includes sensation melodramas, apocalyptic melodramas, fairy-tale melodramas, nautical melodramas, domestic melodramas, gothic melodramas—*and* the moral reform melodrama.[3] While all of these discrete types might be said to embody and reinforce values, and hence deserve to be regarded as "not only a moralistic drama, but as the drama of morality, it was the *moral reform* melodrama, more than the other forms, that assumed ideological and political significance."[4]

During the nineteenth century the moral reform melodrama abounded both in England and in the United States.[5] In the United Kingdom during the early decades of the nineteenth century, popular melodramatists like Douglas Jerrold, J. B. Buckstone, and John Walker adopted and espoused a variety of causes—from temperance reform, in such dramas as *Fifteen Years of a Drunkard's Life* (c. 1828), *The Bottle* (1847), and *The Drunkard's Children* (1848)—to the plight of England's working poor in plays with titles like *Luke the Laborer* (1826), *The Rent Day* (1832), and *The Factory Girl* (1832); while in America, during the middle years of the century, noted social activists like T. S. Arthur and Harriet Beecher Stowe penned reformist narratives that were quickly adapted for the stage. From the mid-nineteenth century onward hundreds of temperance melodramas, the most popular of which were *The Drunkard* (1844) and an adaptation of Arthur's temperance classic *Ten Nights in a Bar-Room* (1852) took the temperance message to the uneducated masses, while numerous adaptations of *Uncle Tom's Cabin*, arguably the greatest moral reform drama of all time, preached abolition to an equally large theatre audience. Peppered with indictments of slavery like George Harris's rebellious lines—"What right has [my master] to me? I'm as much a man as he is!" and his incendiary declaration, "I'll be free, or die!"—stage versions of *Uncle Tom's Cabin* quickly became recognized as politicized statements as transgressive as Mrs. Stowe's original text.[6]

The emergence of the moral reform drama—the ideal vehicle for disseminating progressive ideology during the middle years of the nineteenth century—was hardly a historical anomaly, for, according to Henry Steele Commager, the antebellum era was the "day of universal reform," a period during which "every institution was called before the bar of reason and of sentiment" to be measured and judged against a hierarchy of truths.[7] Predicated on the Enlightenment belief that human beings are divine, that humankind is perfectible, and that, consequently, no social problem could be considered intractable, nineteenth-century reform was "designed to harmonize man with the [ideal] moral order," to promote and encourage human improvement.[8] This overriding conviction—the belief in humanity's potential perfectibility—led naturally and inexorably to a sentimentalized view of the world—a sentimentalized world reflected in the reformist literature of the antebellum era, the melodrama included.

In the decades leading up to the Civil War, reformist ideology was disseminated and promoted in practically all forms of printed matter, from nonfictional tracts and pamphlets to novels and short fiction; from comedies and tragedies on America's stages to newspapers that spanned the political spectrum. Temperance reform, abolition, women's rights, public education, and a host of other reforms all had their own publications, as did the groups that opposed these reforms. And each vied for recognition and a place in the public forum. It is therefore hardly surprising that during this historical period, according to literary historian David Reynolds, many social texts suddenly "lost their semiotic equivalences and became colored by a radical infusion of the imaginative. [In this process] popular reform literature moved from staid, rational tracts on the remedies of vice to sensational, often highly metaphorical exposés of the perverse results of vice" and came to represent what Michael Denning regards as the paradoxical union of sensational fiction and radical politics.[9] And no text relied more on sensation to spread its progressive ideology than did the moral reform melodrama.

Although characterized as melodrama and lumped with the other variations of the form in conventional theatre histories, moral reform dramas differed markedly from the other types, not only in their ultimate nature but in their intent. During the nineteenth century, literary historian Jane Tomkins asserts, most drama was, by definition, a form of discourse that had *no* designs on influencing the course of events.[10] It made no attempt to change things but merely elected to represent them, and its value lay in its representational nature. In contrast to these purely representational works—which constituted the majority of theatrical offerings—were those dramas whose claim to value lay in their stated intention to influence, often significantly, the course of history, to propose solutions to the problems that shaped a particular historical moment. Frequently these dramas were as ideologically radical as the reforms they espoused: slaves denounced the institution of slavery; laborers went on strike against their employers or smashed the machinery in their factories; prohibition was aggressively advocated nearly seventy years before the passage of the Eighteenth Amendment. These were the plays that have been conveniently clustered under the rubric "moral reform drama"—a construct that, in Foucault's terms, was a "node within a network," a set of works that expressed what lay in the minds of many of their creators' contemporaries, "a set of works that tapped into a storehouse of widely held assumptions."[11]

In his survey of nineteenth-century melodrama and what he terms "the myth of America" Jeffrey Mason argues that melodrama's substructure was essentially conservative, with "little room to denounce an oppressive class or institution."[12] The so-called conventional melodrama, in Mason's opinion, was anything but progressive and hardly the carrier of radical, forward-thinking ideology. This was not the case for the moral reform drama. In fact, as I have already stated, moral reform melodramas rivaled in their progressive ideology the social movements that they mirrored and supported. The so-called women's melodrama, popular during the 1840s and most frequently written under the auspices of the American Female Moral Reform Society and published in its magazine, *The Advocate*, for example, presaged the female political activism that emerged later in the century. As routinely constructed, the women's melodrama, a highly ritualized narrative, published most frequently in the form of a novel or short story, warned of the "blandishments of the city," regarded as a predominantly male bastion, and reinforced the correctness and necessity of rural (that is, feminine) morality. At the center of the melodrama was an innocent, young farm girl described in natural terms, as a delicate flower, a plant rooted in the country, endowed with the love and pride of purity.[13] Into the American Eden where she blissfully resided came the lecherous, sophisticated male. Urban and sexual, he was the "antithesis of the pure and family-rooted daughter. . . . He invaded the female family circle, ripping the flower-like daughter from [her roots] and carrying her off to the city. . . . The young woman's final ruin took place in a town or city governed by commercial values, . . . beyond women's sphere, . . . places of absolute sexual powerlessness and danger for the rural daughter."[14] Given its concentration on vital women's issues and its overt political nature, it is hardly surprising that McConachie should rank *Rosina Meadows* (1834), a prototype for the women's melodrama, alongside *The Drunkard* and *Uncle Tom's Cabin* as one of the most influential moral reform dramas of the century.

It is equally instructive to note how closely the American temperance melodrama followed the dominant ideology of its time. When, for example, the Washingtonian Temperance Movement was in full bloom in the early 1840s, the most famous temperance drama of the decade, *The Drunkard*, depicted a stage alcoholic rescued by a temperance representative who, much like the members of the Washingtonians, walked the streets of America's big cities in search of souls to be reclaimed; a decade later, when prohibition was in vogue, the most popular temperance melodrama was *Ten Nights in a Bar-Room*, which advocated a legal, governmental solution to national intemperance. When Romaine, the temperance advocate in William W. Pratt's stage adaptation of T. S. Arthur's temperance classic *Ten Nights in a Bar-Room* (1858), urges the citizens of fictitious, booze-plagued Cedarville to "cut off the fountain [i.e., the bar-room] and . . . save the young, the innocent, from the powers of evil" by voting for Prohibition, morality is paired with the call to public action, inexorably linking a political issue with a moral stance.[15]

During the era of the Women's Christian Temperance Union's dominance, in such plays that supported the WCTU position as Nellie Bradley's *Marry No Man If He Drinks* (1868), Ida Buxton's *On to Victory* (1887), and Effie Merriman's *The Drunkard's Family* (1898), actresses onstage were heard to echo WCTU president Frances Willard's words that women might "clasp hands in one common effort to protect their homes and loved ones from the ravages of drink," while the Anti-saloon League in the 1890s spawned its own strain of temperance plays.[16]

In a similar vein abolitionism and racial issues, although never as popular a theatrical subject as temperance reform, were examined in a series of progressive plays. *The Escape; or, A Leap to Freedom* (1858) was an indictment of slavery written by an escaped slave, William Wells Brown; *Ossawattomie Brown; or, The Insurrection at Harper's Ferry*, by Mrs. J. C. Swayze, glorified John Brown's attack on Harper's Ferry; J. T. Trowbridge castigated the Fugitive Slave Law in *Neighbor Jackwood* (1857); and three adaptations of Mrs. Stowe's second antislavery novel *Dred*—one by C. W. Taylor, a second version by the actor John Brougham, and a third at Barnum's Museum by H. J. Conway—further espoused the cause of abolition set forth in her landmark novel and the various stage adaptations of it. Mrs. Stowe herself penned a drama, titled *The Christian Slave*, and although it was never formally staged in a theatre, it was read in "proslavery" lecture halls in and around Boston during 1854 and 1855 by Mrs. Mary E. Webb, a free mulatto.[17]

In England an emergent strain of prolabor melodrama that developed before the passage of the Labor Reform Bill of 1832 focused public attention on the sociopolitical situation of the lower classes by introducing into the English domestic melodrama a distinctive subversive tone, a disruptive mode of consciousness, and a rhetoric designed to foreground and accentuate the grim realities, class hatreds, and daily crises routinely encountered by the masses. In *Problems in Materialism and Culture* Raymond Williams even suggests that not only were plays like *The Rent Day* and *The Factory Girl* "open attempts to dramatize a new social consciousness," but like the Sunday papers that were gaining popularity in London in the 1820s and 1830s, they combined "sensation, scandal, and radical politics."[18] Through this "new" strain—the polemical moral reform melodrama—the British theatregoing public was graphically, even brutally, introduced to the everyday hardships suffered by workers and their families at the hands of landlords, factory owners, the liquor industry, class hostilities, a harsh urban environment, and, in some cases, governmental agencies.[19] Featuring peasants, artisans, and other "common" men as heroes who were aligned against upper-class oppressors, British labor plays overtly, violently, and often realistically expressed antiaristocrat, antiemployer, antilandowner, and antiurban sentiments while they simultaneously exposed the era's most serious social ills to public scrutiny. In the opinion of Elaine Hadley this "melodramatic resistance [thus] gave a rational voice and a suffering body to the poor in order to transform their predicament into a recognizable moral force that could participate in public debate. Thereafter, 'Moral Force' became a frequently used term in the [English] anti-Poor Movement."[20]

In their own time moral reform melodramas proved effective propaganda vehicles, both in Great Britain and in the United States, and were utilized as the means of reaching audiences heretofore considered unreachable. In England Buckstone, Jerrold, and other progressive playwrights were writing their reformist works just as the so-called minor theatres like the Coburg, the Britannia, and the Surrey were opening their doors to appeal directly and nearly exclusively to working-class audiences; meanwhile, in America stage versions of *Ten Nights in a Bar-Room*, *Uncle Tom's Cabin*, and other adaptations from the printed page played daily to thousands of uneducated, lower-class patrons who never had, and likely never would, read the serialized or novel versions.

In the case of *Uncle Tom's Cabin*, during the 1850s, adaptations of Mrs. Stowe's famous narrative were staged in Baltimore, Boston, Troy (New York), Philadelphia, New Orleans, Chicago, and Detroit, as well as in its principal site, New York City; and in surveying audiences for these productions critics and casual observers alike were astonished by *Uncle Tom's* power "to elicit sympathy across social divides as the middle classes, promised edification rather than [mere] titillation," entered the theatre in ever-increasing numbers. This is how middle-class commentators found themselves sharing theatrical experience with "Bowery Boys." The same observers were even more astonished when the B'hoys wildly cheered events and "words which would have been hissed down in most public meetings and [have been] coldly received in the churches" — words like George Harris's declaration of freedom and denunciation of slavery in act 1 of Aiken's adaptation.[21]

As Sarah Meer has observed, "Even the scripts produced for museum theaters would have presumed audiences more male, working class, and anti-abolition than Stowe's likely readers." The theatricalization of Stowe's novel and the male audiences it attracted thus ensured that the basic story of Tom, Eliza, Little Eva, and Topsy reached beyond the largely female readership for the printed versions, but even for those who had encountered the novel, dramatizations functioned in part as mediating or exegetic texts, conditioning the way such audiences "read" the original.... The wider assimilation of a sense of Stowe's novel was thus closely dependent on the process of dramatic adaptation, and the plays expanded and altered the meanings of the *Tom* phenomenon. Making *Uncle Tom* theatrical inevitably affected its politics and modified its position on slavery.[22]

The ultimate result of compounding the effect of the novel with that of the various dramatizations of Stowe's narrative was to establish it firmly as an "American Jeremiad"—a "mode of public exhortation... designed to join social criticism to spiritual renewal, public to private identity, the shifting 'signs of the times' to certain traditional... themes and symbols."[23]

But the moral reform melodrama was historically significant for yet another reason: it served as a harbinger of the progressive social criticism commonly associated with the realism that emerged later in the nineteenth century. As Thomas Postlewait contends, historically melodrama and realism developed during roughly the same period. As Postlewait summarizes it, both forms "responded to and were shaped by similar socio-political conditions in the modern industrial and imperial age of nationalism, capitalism, population explosion, urban growth,... massive migrations,... ethnic conflict, authoritarian controls, and terrible wars. Here in these complex conditions both art forms found their many topics and themes."[24] In postulating a similarity in intent between realism and melodrama, Postlewait is ostensibly echoing the words of historian Arthur Schlesinger, who wrote that historically "realism and idealism [i.e., melodrama] were not enemies but allies, and... together they defined the morality of social change."[25] Thus, not only did melodrama and realism emerge and develop at approximately the same time, but they dealt with many of the same social issues, albeit the melodrama presented those issues symbolically.

The moral reform melodrama's message was by no means monolithic, however. While melodramatic conventions may have been readily understood, even by the uneducated, and stereotypes are instantly recognizable expressions of complex clusters of value that convey enormous amounts of cultural information in an extremely condensed form and hence contribute to the reception of any narrative, all too often playwrights' reliance on these conventions muted, or even subverted, a play's central ideological imperative. This resulted, at best, in an ambiguous message, at worst, in a total loss of substantive meaning. Since melodramatic stereotypes "tend to *individualize* issues and hence reduce them to matters of private choice, and where suffering or a social problem could be blamed on the villainy of a single character, there was little room to denounce an oppressive . . . institution."[26] This was certainly the case in the two most popular stage versions of *Uncle Tom's Cabin*—George Aiken's version for the Howard Company at Purdy's National Theatre in New York and H. J. Conway's at Barnum's Museum. In both productions evil was ultimately shifted away from the institution of slavery and embedded in the individual villains of the narrative: Haley, Loker, and, most graphically, Simon Legree. When, near the end of their respective melodramas, Aiken and Conway subjected Legree to the mandatory dictates of poetic justice, they not only punished the individual, but they implied that with Legree's death, somehow the overarching problem had been resolved. Such was *not* the case in Stowe's original narrative, in which Legree—and with him, the institutionalized evil of slavery—remained and continued a systemic routine of torture and human degradation.

In a similar way the incorporation of the "stock" temperance reformer into the plot of a temperance melodrama invariably deflected audience attention from the social impact of intemperance that, like slavery in the abolitionist drama, was a national ubervillain. Once Reneslaw, the temperance representative, enters the action of *The Drunkard,* for example, society as a whole is let off the hook. Instead of a call to action, the message to the audience becomes, "Sit back and relax—the temperance guy will take care of everything."

Equally problematic is the ambiguous role of the nineteenth-century reformer. In retrospect it is not difficult to view the reformer (or at least some reformers) as a cultural imperialist—more eager to paternalistically shape the character and regulate the behavior of the "less fortunate" than to redeem and rehabilitate victims of social change. Furthermore, as David Reynolds has documented in *Beneath the American Renaissance,* writers of reform literature, the drama included, were hardly a monolithic group, as demonstrated by the high degree of ethical fluidity in their work.[27] While many reformers (the so-called conventional reformers) avoided "excessive sensationalism and always emphasize[d] the means by which vice [could] be circumvented or remedied," a second, and often more visible, group (whom Reynolds labels "subversive" reformers) were more interested in creating sensationalist narratives than in eradicating vice and/or injustice. These "reformers," although they publicly claimed to be as interested in the morality of reform as were their more traditional, rationalist brethren, were in fact primarily interested in stimulating audience interest through sensational scenes or events ranging from "the grisly, sometimes perverse results of vice, such as shattered homes, sadomasochistic violence, . . . the disillusioning collapse of romantic ideals," or displays of human degradation and humiliation.[28] The existence of the subversive reformer cast doubt on the ideological legitimacy of some of the century's most famous reformist dramas and served to increase the ambiguity of many moral reform dramas, such as Conway's *Uncle Tom's Cabin*, which began with a plantation scene straight out of the antebellum minstrel show and incorporated a slave auction designed more to show off the talents of black singers and dancers than to depict the horrors of the sale of human beings—scenes hardly written to encourage abolitionist sentiments and activism from audiences.

Although these "deficiencies" may have rendered the moral reform drama somewhat ambiguous and at times limited its efficacy as an ideological message bearer, the nineteenth-century moral reform melodrama, warts and all, remained a "passionate record of the metaphysical and social tensions of America that dramatized the dialectic between doubt and faith. Throughout the century it served as a crucial space in which the cultural, political, and economic exigencies of the century could be played out and transformed into public discourses about issues ranging from the gender-specific dimensions of individual station and behavior" to the emancipation of an entire race of humans.[29] Easy to radicalize, highly programmatic, heuristic and didactic in nature rather than merely mimetic, these plays offered powerful examples of the way a culture, or at least a significant portion of that culture, thinks about itself—the ways that culture has devised for articulating and proposing solutions for the problems that shape a particular historical moment. Viewed from our current perspective, dramas such as *Uncle Tom's Cabin*, *The Drunkard*, *The Rent Day*, and *Ten Nights in a Bar-Room* served as the bearers of a set of national, social, and economic interests—vehicles ideally suited to formulate and disseminate ideological messages while they simultaneously entertained the masses.

Notes

1. Mark Twain, "The Indignity Put upon the Remains of George Holland by the Rev. Mr. Sabine," *Galaxy*, Feb. 1871, 321–22.

2. Peter Brooks, *The Melodramatic Imagination* (New York: Columbia University Press, 1985); David Grimsted, *Melodrama Unveiled: American Theatre and Culture, 1800–1850* (Berkeley: University of California Press, 1968); Bruce A. McConachie, *Melodramatic Formations: American Theatre and Society*,

1820–1870 (Iowa City: University of Iowa Press, 1992); Rosemarie K. Bank, *Theatre Culture in America, 1825–1860* (New York: Cambridge University Press, 1997); Elaine Hadley, *Melodramatic Tactics: Theatricalized Dissent in the English Marketplace, 1800–1885* (Stanford, CA: Stanford University Press, 1995).

3. McConachie, *Melodramatic Formations*, 6.

4. This is a distillation of Peter Brooks's description in Brooks, *The Melodramatic Imagination*, ix–xvi, 1–35.

5. Although British reform and those melodramas that supported it will not be the prime focus here, I mention them because there are distinct parallels between American and English reform melodramas in both intent and effect.

6. George Aiken, *Uncle Tom's Cabin*, in *Dramas from the American Theatre, 1792–1909*, ed. Richard Moody (New York: Houghton Mifflin, 1966), 360–61.

7. Henry Steele Commager, *The Era of Reform, 1830–1860* (Princeton, NJ: D. Van Nostrand, 1960), 8–9.

8. Ibid., 9.

9. David S. Reynolds, *Beneath the American Renaissance: The Subversive Imagination in the Age of Emerson and Melville* (Cambridge, MA: Harvard University Press, 1988), 7; Michael Denning, *Mechanics Accents: Dime Novels and Working-Class Culture in America* (London: Verso, 1987), 87.

10. Jane P. Tompkins, *Sensational Designs: The Cultural Work of American Fiction, 1790–1860* (New York: Oxford University Press, 1985), 125.

11. Quoted in ibid., xv–xvi.

12. Quoted in Sarah Meer, *Uncle Tom Mania: Slavery, Minstrelsy, and Transatlantic Culture in the 1850s* (Athens: University of Georgia Press, 2005), 109.

13. Carroll Smith-Rosenberg, "Misprisoning Pamela: Representations of Gender and Class in Nineteenth-Century America," *Michigan Quarterly Review* 26 (winter 1987): 14.

14. Ibid.

15. William W. Pratt, *Ten Nights in a Bar-Room* (New York, c. 1858), 44.

16. The source of all temperance information in this paper is from John W. Frick, *Theatre, Culture, and Temperance Reform in Nineteenth-Century America* (New York: Cambridge University Press, 2003). The Willard quotation is cited on p. 165.

17. Ibid., 58.

18. Raymond Williams, *Problems in Materialism and Culture* (London: Verso, 1980), 134–35.

19. Jim Davis, "Melodrama, Community, and Ideology: London's Minor Theatres in the Nineteenth Century," paper presented at the melodrama conference, Institute of Education, London, 1992, 1; Michael Hays, "To Delight and Discipline: Melodrama as Cultural Mediator," paper presented at the melodrama conference, Institute of Education, London, 1992, 6.

20. Hadley, *Melodramatic Tactics*, 99.

21. Meer, *Uncle Tom Mania*, 107–11.

22. Ibid., 111, 105.

23. Sacvan Bercovitch, *The American Jeremiad* (Madison: University of Wisconsin Press, 1978), quoted in Tompkins, *Sensational Designs,* 140.

24. Thomas Postlewait, "From Melodrama to Realism: The Suspect History of American Drama," in *Melodrama: The Cultural Emergence of a Genre,* ed. Michael Hays and Anastasia Nikolopoulou (New York: St. Martin's, 1996), 54.

25. Arthur Schlesinger, *The American as Reformer* (New York: Athenaeum, 1968), xiii.

26. Mason quoted in Meer, *Uncle Tom Mania,* 109; see also Tompkins, *Sensational Designs,* xvi.

27. Reynolds, *Beneath the American Renaissance,* 59.

28. Ibid., 39.

29. Michael Hays and Anastasia Nikolopoulou, introduction to *Melodrama: The Cultural Emergence of a Genre,* ed. Michael Hays and Anastasia Nikolopoulou (New York: St. Martin's, 1996), viii; Reynolds, *Beneath the American Renaissance,* 76.

Tainted Money?

Nineteenth-Century Charity Theatricals

Eileen Curley

IN THE LATTER HALF of the nineteenth century, treading onto a public stage in New York City was still seen as an immoral choice for a woman of society, and the occasional amateur who "went pro" was roundly criticized and often disowned by her family. Yet as amateur theatricals grew in popularity and the performers and audiences outgrew parlors, some aspiring actors found a way to exploit social constructions of gender roles and gain public performance opportunities under the guise of propriety: the charity theatrical. Theatricals, like charity concerts and readings, quickly became a fashionable way to raise money not only for the financially or morally bereft but for military units, collegiate athletic teams, churches, the Statue of Liberty, and an endless variety of clubs. The events were purported to be an evening dedicated to some good fun for the sake of a deserving charity. Beneath the surface, however, the import of these productions appears significantly less simplistic or easily resolved.

Charity theatricals, as one segment of postwar benevolent activity, were simply one of many ways that women were able to use their revered and cultivated parlor skills to display their talents outside of the living room. Theatre, however, has historically maintained a morally ambiguous place in society, and theatricals have historically been the most problematic of women's living-room entertainments; therefore, theatricals were burdened with an extra layer of moral ambiguity from which singing and handiwork seemed immune, even when those talents were displayed publicly in concerts and fairs. By performing charity theatricals in rented halls and public theatres, the social elite managed to engage in morally questionable behavior while maintaining an outward display of propriety. In a society that associated charity work with middle- and upper-middle-class femininity and public performance with the morally questionable acting profession, a charity theatrical, for women, became a moral display of femininity via a potentially immoral act. No longer safely ensconced in the parlors of their fathers and husbands, women subjected themselves to public scrutiny by both the audience and newspaper reviewers. Yet the widespread advertising and puffing of some theatricals suggest that a condoned display of self was now expanding beyond parlors, society balls, and the society pages. Clearly, charity theatricals provided a sanctioned way for dramatically inclined members of the middle and upper class to display their talents on a public stage, but could simply sending the proceeds of the event to a charity protect the participants from being tainted by their activities?

The history of charity theatricals in the United States is difficult to chart. In New York, at least, a dearth of public notices about charity theatricals before the Civil War seems to support an 1855 *New York Times* observation that Americans had yet to widely adopt the British fashion of charity theatricals. "It is rather remarkable, that with our aptitude for imitating our trans-Atlantic neighbors, we have never followed the fashion which has prevailed in England the past ten years, of giving private theatricals for the benefit of charitable institutions." The article goes on to credit Charles Dickens with "converting these harmless recreations to benevolent purposes," and it suggests that the popularity of his charity theatricals created something of a fad for them in England.[1]

This growth in charity theatricals necessarily requires a private theatrical infrastructure, so it is not surprising that England came to charity theatricals before the United States did. Private theatricals have a long history as entertainment for the upper classes in England, but the first widespread evidence of their popularity in the United States emerges in the middle years of the nineteenth century. While it appears that private theatricals were growing in popularity prior to the Civil War, these events were largely confined to spaces with restricted access and appear to have been held for charitable benefit only rarely.[2] Two different but closely related postwar performance trends developed slowly—charity theatricals and public presentations of theatricals—and the popularity of the one seems to have fed that of the other.[3] As such, a marked increase in charity theatricals occurs slightly before the new trend for public presentations of theatricals, the latter certainly driven by the novelty of charity theatricals, the need for fund-raising in the postwar economy, and the availability of performance spaces, such as club theatres, outside of the family parlor. By the 1870s, "charity" became an excuse to stage a "private" theatrical in a rented public hall or commercial theatre, as well as in more selective club theatres.[4]

Although the audiences for charity theatricals were likely self-selecting, the performers had significantly less control over their audiences than in a truly "private" theatrical. Tickets were often publicly advertised as being on sale at bookstores, hotels, and the private residences of patronesses—and while the patronesses in particular might have limited their sales to respectable audience members, the public sale of tickets necessarily opened the events to audiences beyond the performer's regular social circle. Even the patroness system resulted in audience members who were unknown to the performers, as Rita Lawrence explains in her recounting of a charity event: "the tickets had only been sent to people of good standing, though many (as usual in these charity affairs) not known to us or our friends."[5] Anyone could, in theory, attend a publicly advertised charity theatrical, provided they could afford the ticket and were willing to watch amateur performers. Even as early as 1855, the *New York Times* acknowledged that "private theatricals . . . is not the proper name for them, as they are open to the public" when staged for charity.[6] While charity theatricals did occur in private homes, and while the reporting of such events was likely limited, as Lawrence suggests,[7] hundreds of charity events in the period bore a closer resemblance to a public commercial theatre production than their parlor counterparts simply because of their performance for a general paying audience. As such, charity theatricals represent an uneven demarcation line in the history of amateur theatre in the United States. This gradual shift out of parlors and into public spaces was at once enabled by and intertwined with developments in benevolent activity, and these developments shared many of the same implications for postwar ideas of femininity. By granting women the power to reform society through benevolent causes, society also permitted, and indeed encouraged, female activity beyond the spheres of life normally permissible by social constructions of femininity.

Charity theatricals, as one of numerous postwar charitable activities, were part of a larger tradition of philanthropic behavior in the United States, and even though neither the tradition nor the theatricals were uniquely associated with women, gender played a large role in the development of both. Although modern scholarship has done much to disprove the actual legitimacy of the "cult of true womanhood," the society that created that cultural myth was, in fact, the same society that permitted and, indeed, encouraged women to participate in benevolent activities by linking those events so clearly with ideals of femininity. Women, in addition to being considered more sensitive and emotive than their male counterparts, were generally believed to possess a greater capacity for moral and religious behavior and, in turn, were charged with protecting the morality of society. Theoretically, as women were naturally inclined to be morally upright caretakers who were resistant to the evils of the world, they could be natural reformers who could model proper behavior and lead others to a virtuous life.

G. J. Barker-Benfield successfully illuminates the philosophical and theoretical groundwork that underlies the association of philanthropy, gender, and sensibility in the late eighteenth- and nineteenth-century United States. Sensibility became particularly associated with women because of their perceived biological weaknesses, but it is the growth of the culture of sensibility alongside the growth of consumer culture that enables Barker-Benfield to link female sensibility with philanthropic giving in this period. The growth of consumer culture allowed "[b]ourgeois Anglo-American white women . . . to enter a new public world of formal visits, pleasure gardens, shopping parades, assembly rooms, and theaters of the 'urban renaissance'—spaces intended for the enjoyment and cultivation of new heterosocial manners, including their tasteful expressions of sensibility."[8] Yet this very wealth and freedom came at the expense of the workers, whose labor permitted the industrial revolution and slave trade to turn a profit. "In short, as commercial capitalists and then industrial capitalists helped to create prosperity by immiserating millions, they also helped to elaborate a consumer society nourishing the possibilities for the aggrandizement of the interior life, the elevation of feelings."[9] For women, their increased capacity for sensibility and their central presence in the domestic sphere, which existed in large part as a result of the consumer revolution, made them logically empowered philanthropists; they had the free time and empathetic capacity to feel the pain of others and to act on it. "Middle class women exerted social power for themselves and their male collaborators, helping to generate their own collectivity, as it were, in dispensing tea and sympathy, whence they brought criticism to bear on the world of unfeeling men."[10] It was, of course, that "world of unfeeling men" that simultaneously permitted women the economic position to help and yet refused them the power to prevent the social ills from existing in the first place. Indeed, women of this period can be read either as social pawns who attempted to clean up after the male establishment's industrial messes or as a subversive force that sought to undermine established authority by using the fruits of its labor to help those in need and by using the assumptions of gendered sensibility to gain a public voice through philanthropic giving.

Prior to the Civil War this link between gender roles and benevolence existed within a philanthropic tradition that was, Wendy Gamber argues, as much about self-reform as about reforming others. She suggests that "almost all antebellum reformers shared certain fundamental beliefs: Almost all believed that it was possible not only to change the world, but also to perfect it."[11] Thus, despite wide-ranging ideals that produced temperance societies, abolitionist groups, and utopian communities, these reformers sought to improve their world and themselves according to their ideals, and they saw little difference between reforming themselves and philanthropic giving to another.[12] Reformers, more often than not, took their own advice and sought to better their own lives by, for example, giving up drinking or joining utopian communities. Gamber suggests that the vibrancy of many of the antebellum movements began to wane by the 1850s, and these idealistic dreams were often replaced with a focus on more practical social troubles and an accompanying split between reformer and recipient.[13]

Philanthropy in the postwar era, when charity theatricals became popular, was largely marked by this concern with helping others without necessarily improving oneself in the process. The differences between benefactor and beneficiary became more clearly delineated, and the social ills to which postwar women devoted their time were more likely to be social ills that they, the benefactors, did not encounter in their own upper- or middle-class lives. For theatricals, in particular, this separation between self and method of reform reduced the potential that the charity theatricals might have been seen as providing the performers with, such as an opportunity to reform their elocutionary skills or public presence. This self-improvement through performance, a common refrain in guidebooks which sought to ameliorate concern over the morality of theatricals, rarely appears in reference to charity theatricals, except insofar as talented amateurs used these performances as a stepping stone to an even more immoral act: going pro.

Indeed, early charity theatricals are marked instead by the latter component of Gamber's observation: a clear differentiation between those who are economically positioned to help and those who need their assistance. Charity theatricals also provided participants with the ability to assist the impoverished without necessarily having to physically encounter the orphaned children or working girls whose lives the performers sought to improve. Women were able to continue to hold their roles as moral guardians by helping those who were less fortunate through fund-raising activities that never took them beyond their own social spheres or comfort zones.

In addition to reaffirming social class barriers while underscoring the economic differences between the participants and those in need, charity theatricals appear to have served a dual purpose for the participants—fund-raising and leisure entertainment. Middle- and upper-class women had a unique combination of leisure time and financial capital that allowed them time to stage elaborate theatricals and to perform charity work simultaneously. Concurrently, through theatricals society granted women the permission to act out of bounds while still acting well within accepted power structures and cultural norms. While living-room theatricals appear to have had fairly short rehearsal periods, extant records of charity theatricals, particularly the well-advertised ones for flashier causes, suggest a much greater attention to rehearsal and production. These extensive preparations also imply a greater focus on aesthetic quality than might be the object of a parlor performance, but this focus on producing a quality performance also aligns the charity theatrical more closely with commercial theatre. Good intentions did not always lead to success, however, and this dual purpose of leisure and fund-raising left the performers open to multiple conflicting interpretations of their public behavior.

Indeed, charity theatricals presented direct counterpoints to the nineteenth-century ideologies that linked women with benevolence and presumed that women were natural caretakers who lived to do little else. Lori Ginzberg argues that "[t]he success of charitable and benevolent endeavors depended on this belief in women's invisibility and lack of self-interest."[14] Just as the amateurs sought to distance themselves from commercial theatre by creating carefully nuanced distinctions between the two sets of activities, so did charitable organizations rely on public perceptions to influence the direction of society's moral compass. Groups with the financial and societal power to assist the morally or financially impoverished did so in part to shape the course of society, but Ginzberg argues that women's key role in benevolent giving permitted the appearance of unselfish action while simultaneously allowing for public recognition of the results of those actions:

> Charity cannot be wholly invisible if it is to make these lessons clear. Women or, more accurately, the belief in women's moral superiority perfectly fit the requirement that charitable endeavors appear unmotivated by self- or class interest. As members of a group that seemed to be defined exclusively by gender, women could have no interest other than to fulfill their benevolent destiny; they could be applauded and recognized without calling into question the purity of their motives.[15]

Within such a public-relations framework charity theatricals might have been much like any other charitable event wherein women would work together solely for the sake of the poor. In reality, however, we have far too many references to women's love of acting and performing to maintain such a naive outlook on the supposedly pure motives of the performers. Charity theatricals, particularly those with extravagant financial outlays and extensive rehearsals, advertising, and puffing, hardly permitted the women to remain even metaphorically invisible. Rather, their angelic selves appeared onstage before thousands of potentially unknown audience members who had paid to see the performance. The associations between charity and commercial performers were underscored by the performance of popular plays, in full costume, with rented or custom sets (occasionally those used in commercial performances) in commercial theatres.

The potentially problematic public display of self on the stage appears to have been tempered somewhat by the mechanisms of charitable organizations, as well as by the production traditions of the amateur companies. Much of the early movement out of parlors and into public spaces was aided by the growth and development of dramatic and nondramatic clubs and organizations. Theatricals staged by a club or group became a reflection on the entity, much as parlor theatricals were seen as a reflection on the family (or the father figure). In all but a few notable cases it appears that the primary focus of theatricals remained squarely on the charity or the organization that produced the event, not on any individual stars. Amateur performers, then, were not often subjected to the acclaim or the notoriety of professional actors within the star system.[16] This seemingly minor distinction between amateur and professional performer parallels and reflects the at best contradictory nature of women's power in benevolent giving as well.

Public perceptions of acting also serve to differentiate the amateurs from their professional counterparts. Socially, amateur performers believed that they occupied the moral high ground when compared to professional actors, much as they occupied the financial and moral high ground when compared to the beneficiaries that they assisted through theatricals.[17] Theatrically, training and talent served to differentiate even the most renowned amateur from a professional counterpart. Authors of guidebooks for amateur theatricals routinely reminded their readers that not everyone could act well and that amateurs should not strive to perform above their talent level. The guides' discussions about acting seemed intended to keep the amateur's focus on the communal fun that might be had through theatricals and, perhaps more important, to reinforce that it took talent and training to be treated as a professional actor and to stage aesthetically successful productions that could compare with the commercial stage the amateurs sought to emulate. Hence, the guidebooks, with their insistence on acting as a learned skill and not solely as a naturally occurring talent, seem to release the amateurs from any taint of professionalism while centering the focus of the events on the charitable action and not the aesthetic quality of the performance.[18]

The coverage of charity theatricals in the newspapers of the day responded to their growth in popularity, resulting in the growth of actual performance reviews. Amateur actors appear to have been tolerated by most reviewers, who seemed capable of recognizing the place that amateur theatricals held in society. Weaknesses in shows were expected, further reinforcing the differences between the amateurs' and professionals' skills: "Like most amateur efforts, however, they are deficient in the very points that make the difference between the effort and the accomplishment."[19] Hence, while many felt that "[t]he ordinary amateur actor is a nuisance and a useless vanity, and when seen in public he cuts a sorry figure,"[20] they kept critiques of such poor performances sufficiently vague as to keep their readership pleased. The argument that "[s]tringent criticism would . . . be out of place" held sway for quite some time, as did the notion that "the efforts of unprofessional actors rarely are interesting except to their prejudiced friends."[21] As amateur theatricals became more common, reviewers often did single out performers, and would note which members of the cast were frequent performers or routinely successful, but would usually refrain from offering criticisms of a named performer. Some truly horrid productions were not even listed by club name or performance name on occasion, instead left to pass on into the ephemeral history of amateur theatre, hopefully to be soon forgotten by all involved.

Commentary on the appropriateness of a particular play chosen for amateur representation occasionally appears in reviews, but theatricals were not often publicly judged on their play selection. A review of the February 7, 1872, production of *All That Glitters Is Not Gold*, by the Murray Hill Amateur Dramatic Association, notes that it is a play "with a fine, wholesome moral,"[22] but the reviewer's discussion focused, as was typical, on the performance itself and not on the plot of the play. Thus it stands to reason that while the selection of the play might have been seen as important for the guidebook authors who routinely emphasized the selection of "appropriate" plays, it seldom seemed to matter to the reviewers.[23] The extent to which the amateurs took the advice of the guides and hence were spared harsh commentary will never be truly known, although amateurs did show a propensity for performing comedies, gentlemanly melodramas, and musicals. Despite these tendencies, little was seen as off-limits to amateurs, who performed minstrel shows, vaudeville shows, operas, burlesques, and occasionally Shakespeare. As the *New York Times* noted in 1886, as theatricals became more acceptable and more amateurs began acting in public, their choices of plays drifted further and further away from those suggested by the guidebooks: "The number of amateur actors is constantly increasing; in the neighboring town of Brooklyn, there are a dozen dramatic societies, we believe, the members of which tackle the blank verse drama, prose comedy, romantic and sensational drama, pastoral-comical, historical-pastoral, scene individable [*sic*] or poem unlimited to their own satisfaction and the delight of their relatives and friends."[24] This particular review goes on to note that many performers were less than successful, aesthetically, in their theatricals. Hence, while the amateurs certainly observed few limits when choosing plays, they might have been well served to avoid some plays or perhaps to avoid acting altogether. Yet the guise of charity again seems to have negated or at least excused poor productions, be they due to acting or play selection.

Poor reviews and the guidebooks' suggestions to "be appropriate" did little to dampen the enthusiasm for amateur theatricals in the period. If anything, it seems that subpar performances were to be expected, and good acting was often singled out with astonishment, at least in the early years. Some troupes of amateur performers, like the Strollers or the Amaranth, became known for producing quality amateur productions for charity and hence were able to raise more money through multiple-night shows than other groups, but these groups represented the upper echelon of the amateur acting pool and often produced amateurs who turned professional because, in part, of their successes on the amateur stage. If anything, the success of these well-regarded societies seems to have inspired other groups, some of whom went so far as to borrow journeyman amateur actors for performances. A lack of aesthetic success, however, did not seem to matter much for the smaller groups, as the focus of those events was never clearly placed on theatrical skill. For better or worse the charity would benefit from the efforts of the amateurs, and the countless slights about amateur acting that pervade the newspapers of the time seem to suggest that watching poor performances was the price one paid for performing a charitable deed.

Positive reviews, on the contrary, presented the largest danger to an amateur's moral and social standing, not because of the praise itself but because of the feared potential outcome that it might produce. Amateurs in charity events were expected to remain largely anonymous parts of the entire performance event. It was feared that when reviewers singled out an amateur for praise, that solo recognition for a talented, albeit amateur, performance would lead the amateur to become indecorously vain. Vanity, in turn, might lead the amateur to attempt to turn professional, thereby causing the performer to potentially damage her reputation by taking to the commercial stage. Hence, when the focus of the charity theatrical was placed on the aesthetics of the event and not on the charitable aspects of it, the danger posed to the morality of the participants was greater, in part because of the potential that amateur performance had, at least in the eyes of fearful parents and husbands, to inspire women to forgo their place in society and turn professional.

Yet the structures of charitable organizations and the postwar trends in benevolence served to protect or restrict women from acquiring the solo public voice that seems to be one of the minute points that protected amateurs from the taint of public performance. Despite being a socially sanctioned part of nineteenth-century femininity, benevolent activity allowed women of the upper and middle classes to assume a power and authority that normally would not have been extended to them. Socially, this power was not granted to the individual woman but rather to a group or charitable organization.[25] Kathleen McCarthy traces the development of such groups between 1790 and 1860, noting that the growth during this period provides the foundation for postwar charitable giving. She argues that "once they gathered together to form a legally chartered charitable corporation, even married women assumed a part of a collective identity that imbued them with legal prerogatives that they lacked as individuals, including the right to buy, sell, and invest [in] property and to sign binding contracts."[26] By working in groups to fund organizations that set about to reform society, these women could work to reform social ills, and in doing so, the women's groups gained political and societal power.[27] By choosing which charities to support, the women could determine which problems received attention and thereby influence public policy through their work at a time when they could not do so through the ballot box.

The women's power was also derived from their social class. Charity theatricals, like much postwar benevolent activity, were marked by a clear differentiation between those with economic positions of power and those who needed their assistance. In the case of theatricals, however, women transgressed acceptable theatrical boundaries while fulfilling their roles as moral caretakers.

Groups of middle- and upper-class women did much of the organizing and patronizing of charity theatricals, reflecting the postwar organization-based approach to philanthropy. Amateur dramatic societies appear and disappear with great regularity in the late nineteenth century, yet most early groups appear to either be wholly devoted to charity, as in the case of the Charity Amateur Dramatic Association and the Ladies Dramatic Union, or at least regularly involved in charitable events. In the 1860s, while individual families or groups of friends would often stage theatricals in their homes and send a notice of the event to the society pages, it was rare to find a named organization staging a theatrical in a public venue for anything other than charitable purposes. Likewise, when friends grouped together to stage a theatrical in a public venue, there was almost always a beneficiary, at least in the 1860s and 1870s.

The Murray Hill Amateur Dramatic Association, active in theatricals in the early 1870s, routinely held benefit performances, but reports of its 1872 performance for the New York Infant Asylum are particularly reflective of many trends in postwar charitable giving. The *New York Times* preview article about the March 21 performance "earnestly entreat[s] our theatre-going readers" to purchase tickets for the production for the sake of the children and to help the organizers achieve their goal:

> The immediate object of the benevolent ladies who manage the charity is to raise a sum of money sufficient to build a suitable edifice in the country to which the children, or a part of them, may be removed.... [A]s soon as the weather gets warm, a large fraction of their number, we are assured, are certain to die.... Two dollars is no great sum to part with; yet it may, at this juncture, be the means of saving a human life. We beg all who can [to] make this trifling outlay for the sake of the poor little waifs who are so unhappily abandoned, and for that of the noble-hearted women to whom the success of the charity is very dear.

Herein, the idealistic association of women as caregivers to young, helpless children is more than evident. The melodramatic positioning of the children in death's grip enables the Murray Hill Amateur Dramatic Association managers to be clearly differentiated from the scalawag parents of the orphans. The ladies are "noble-hearted women" whose hard work for the pitiful children should be supported and idealized, much as the women themselves are idealized in this article. The extensive discussion of the children clearly places the focus of the event on the fund-raising and the beneficiaries, not on the acting or the performance. Indeed, the play title appears in none of the articles about this event. Even the remark that people should "buy a ticket, whether able to go to the Thursday performance or not," suggests that the focus of the event is, above all, on raising money for the children.[28]

The exact system through which a benefactor was chosen for individual events remains unclear. Certainly, the choice of beneficiary reflected on the participants, and occasionally there were clear links between the benefactors and the beneficiaries. The Ladies Dramatic Union tended to assist charities devoted to helping those of the Jewish faith, and numerous individual churches or church groups held theatricals for the benefit of either their own institution or the poor in their neighborhood. Homes for newsboys, working girls, and orphans were popular beneficiaries, as were churches and hospitals. It seems, however, that sometimes a beneficiary could apply for assistance from a dramatic club. This approach, presumably, is why the Students' Dramatic Club advertised for "applications from charitable organizations for benefit performances" at the end of a review of their May 1894 performances of *The Organist* and *Nita's First*.[29]

Fashionable causes also provided performance opportunities, and the exhortations for financial support for public artworks such as the fund for the pedestal of the Statue of Liberty served as the cause célèbre for numerous theatricals in the mid-1880s. In the late nineteenth century, many public monuments were erected to glorify and embody the ideals of the newly reunited country. "Champions of the republican ideals of liberty and equality looked on public monuments as a vital means of communicating the values of a popular government to large numbers of people."[30] By joining in the fund-raising for public artworks, the participants clearly aligned themselves with the ideologies associated with the particular artworks. This transference of meaning from the beneficiary to the benefactor in the case of public art creates a subtly different relationship between the charity performer and the object of the efforts. The women who organized the charity theatricals to raise money for the Pedestal Fund were raising funds for a statue that represented liberties that they did not themselves possess. Babcock and Macaloon's description of the Statue of Liberty's dedication ceremony reinforces the ironically complicated positioning of the women who performed for the sake of the statue: "As the suffragettes who circled Bedloe's Island in a boat at the dedication announced on a megaphone, if Liberty got down off her pedestal, she would not have been allowed to vote in either France or America—let alone attend her own unveiling ceremony."[31] Charitable activities and amateur performances certainly granted the women some transgressive liberties, but here again we have another example of women who worked within the cultural system of charity theatricals to exploit their own gender roles and significance while simultaneously reinforcing the very foundational support for their subjugation.

The amateurs who staged charity theatricals for the Bartholdi Pedestal

Fund were following in the footsteps of the commercial theatre, not simply by performing theatricals but by performing publicly advertised theatricals for the benefit of the fund. When the initial call for fundraising went out in 1882, Wallack, Frohman, Abbey, and Palmer all volunteered to hold benefit events at their respective theatres.[32] A professional production of Miss Jean Burnside's *Was He Right?* at the Academy of Music on February 3, 1883, was organized by a group of women associated with the Bartholdi Statue Committee. Their efforts at attracting notable society members to attend the event were evidenced by long published lists of box-holders and a *New York Times* commentary that "[i]t is doubtful if the notable assemblage could have been brought together by the merits of the play."[33] Within weeks the amateurs were no longer gathering audiences for professional productions but were instead organizing the first of many amateur productions to benefit the fund.

Mrs. James Brown Potter and her cadre of loyal amateur performers staged a series of theatricals for the benefit of the Bartholdi Pedestal Fund on April 24, 25, and 26, 1883. These theatricals appear to have been akin to other highly organized events and seem to have spared no expense in detail or planning. The managers hired The Madison Square Theatre, acquired costumes used in that season's Vanderbilt Ball, and, according to Charles Crandall, "[t]he programmes, which were donated by Tiffany & Co., were neatly engraved, and bore a relief in gilt of the statue. They were tied each day with different colored ribbons." The matinee performance bills included Frank Harvey's *The Old Love and the New* and a dramatization of Tennyson's "Princess" by a Professor Shields. During the "Princess," Mrs. Brown Potter, "sitting on a throne, wearing a sleeveless, creamy-colored robe and a student's cap [delivered a] spirited declamation of Tennyson's woman's rights sentiments." Crandall notes that "[t]he managers felt sure of realizing a good sum from the performance, thus giving the fund a good start before, as Mrs. Potter says in her epilogue, 'leaving the men to do the rest.'"[34]

Indeed, her positioning as a beautiful classically inspired woman in possession of little actual worldly power allowed Mrs. Brown Potter to be a living embodiment of "Liberty Enlightening the World." Despite Crandall's assessment, the text was hardly a rallying cry for women's rights but rather a recasting of traditional gender roles that parallels Liberty's and the performer's own troubled semiotic meanings. Certainly, the women were acting outside of bounds by performing, but their true power ends before they can fully act, for the men have "to do the rest" and actually use the fruits of the fund-raising and the performing to create a truly public artwork. Women's volition and their creative powers, as with all amateur theatricals, stop just short of providing an unhindered public opportunity for artistic creation and displays of power. Instead, the ladies must work within the frameworks of charitable organizations while performing male idealizations of their character in efforts to establish what was "the world's largest female monument"[35] and, as such, an enormous masculine appropriation of and interpretation of femininity: Bartholdi's statue of "Liberty Enlightening the World."

The spring of 1884 found Mrs. Brown Potter and her friends again planning a series of February theatricals and tableaux for the fund, but their efforts were not widely echoed by other amateur groups until after Joseph Pulitzer began his repeated badgering of the public on March 17, 1885, in the pages of his *New York World*.[36] Numerous charitable organizations and amateur performance groups answered his rallying cry with fairs, exhibits, theatricals, and donations. Fund-raisers varied in both content and participants: Company I of the Seventh Regiment of the New York State National Guard performed *Box and Cox* and a burlesque of *The Lady of Lyons* on April 13 and 14,[37] while rumors circulated that organizers of an April 26 performance of *The Romance of a Poor Young Man* for the benefit of the Boys' Club of St. George's Church should stage the production during the upcoming social season in Washington, DC, for the benefit of the Bartholdi Pedestal Fund.[38] The fund also attracted combined group efforts. As was occasionally seen in other charity theatricals for notable causes, groups of amateurs joined forces for this charity, and in doing so created more of a stir than might otherwise have occurred. By choosing a minstrel show format, the organizers of the May 8, 1885, benefit entertainment at the Academy of Music allowed for easy blending of multiple groups, ranging from members of the Columbia College and Seventh Regiment Glee Clubs to members of amateur dramatic societies. While the audiences would still necessarily be self-selecting, the breadth of participants, number of influential patronesses, and the attendance of theatre parties ensured successful ticket sales and fund-raising.[39]

The nationalistic fervor that accompanied the Bartholdi statue events did appear in fund-raising drives for public artworks like the Grant Monument, even if the latter was not as much of a cause célèbre. The *New York Times* put out calls in the fall of 1885 for contributions to the Grant Monument fund, explicitly requesting that society members solicit contributions from social events and implying that their support of the fund was an appropriate form of patriotism. "Certainly no worthier cause for the labor of men and women can be suggested than that of rearing to the memory of America's great hero a memorial which shall fittingly commemorate his deeds and character."[40] Throughout this editorial leisure-time social events and national pride are linked together through a type and amount of charitable giving that is clearly associated with the upper classes who participate in the social season. "Collections made at tea parties and receipts from amateur theatricals and other social entertainments may be made before the end of the season to increase the fund to an extent which cannot be estimated in advance."[41] The World of Society column made a direct appeal to all of the participants in 1885 theatricals for the Bartholdi Pedestal Fund, exhorting them to "consider the feasibility of giving *The Mikado* by amateurs for this popular fund."[42] In February 1886 a group of women answered the paper's call and, "determined to show that they could do something to indicate their patriotism, have been for some time past laboring to get up a theatrical performance for the benefit of the Grant Monument fund."[43] Their chosen play was *Richard III*, perhaps not the most flattering of choices for the fund, but the play appears to have been selected because the cast had "acted in it before with success,"[44] and the production could presumably be counted on to raise a substantial amount of money.

Comparatively few published accounts of theatricals for other public artworks have been found, particularly when compared to the extensive coverage of the Bartholdi Pedestal Fund theatricals. The disparity seems understandable, given that the Bartholdi statue's fund-raising became Joseph Pulitzer's pet project to raise donations, as well as the reputation of his *New York World*. Quietly advertised events for the Soldiers' Monument Fund in 1879 and Gottschalk statue in 1870 had neither the fanfare nor the public appeal, it seems, that accompanied the Bartholdi Pedestal Fund.[45] Even the Grant Monument's fund-raising, begun in earnest shortly after his death in the summer of 1885 and with lofty aims of raising one million dollars, could not rival that of the Statue of Liberty. Sufficiently powerful society members were associated with both causes, yet one wonders if the overlapping fund-raising drives, weariness from sustained fund-raising for the Bartholdi Pedestal Fund, a much higher price tag, and a lack of a finalized design ultimately rendered the Grant Monument a less-worthy charitable cause.[46] Certainly, the Bartholdi fund-raising was widespread and lasted for nearly three years, with even professional theatres and performers donating proceeds from specially advertised charity performances. Notably, this connection between amateur and professional performers seemed to cause little uproar in certain circles, as the charitable events continued, often housed in the same theatres, until the fund reached its goal of $250,000 in 1885.

The funds raised by the charity theatricals vary widely, but it was not uncommon for a theatrical in the 1880s to take in more than one thousand dollars, and the 1884 productions for the Bartholdi fund by Mrs. Brown Potter were expected to bring in twenty-five hundred dollars.[47] The Ladies' Dramatic Union staged an immensely successful production of *Iolanthe* on March 29, 1884, and sold six thousand dollars' worth of tickets for the Home for Chronic Invalids.[48] By 1899 a performance of *The Lady from Chicago* by the Strollers, one of the more prestigious clubs in New York, took in a reported twenty thousand dollars.[49] Although the latter staggering amount may be anomalous, the charity theatrical remained a solid means of fund-raising. Even without donations, events with limited seating could turn a sizable profit based solely on ticket sales, for ticket scalping was not unheard of. Tickets for the February 4, 1885, benefit performance of *Fair Weather and Foul*, held in Mrs. William C. Whitney's tapestry salon, were in such demand that some of the three hundred tickets, which had originally sold for three dollars apiece, were going for twenty dollars apiece outside the house.[50]

This tradition of helping the less fortunate does not characterize all charity theatricals in the period. As the century progressed, more and more groups began to hold events for the benefit of their own organizations, just as more and more theatricals were held without even the protective guise of "charitable" behavior. By the 1880s, increasing numbers of theatricals appear to have been staged in public venues either completely without designated beneficiaries or with what were, at best, sketchy ones. As a result the semblance of propriety and social justice that provided the socially approved foundation for earlier public performances was utterly lacking from many events in the 1880s and 1890s.

Even for those theatricals that still had beneficiaries, the call to improve society appears to have been answered with much less frequency as the century drew to a close. Impoverished children were often forgotten and replaced by rowing paraphernalia. Athletic clubs, in particular, seemed to have caught on to the fund-raising possibilities of theatricals, and they often staged events to benefit their own clubs. For example, the Staten Island Cricket Club performed *Caste* on June 16, 1885, because it needed to raise funds to move the club after the land was sold out from under it.[51] Columbia's and Harvard's athletic teams appear to have been particularly needy in the latter part of the century, and the North Shore Ladies Tennis Club staged a November 1886 theatrical for the benefit of the Ladies' Tennis Club of the Staten Island Cricket Club.[52]

While the often scarce extant documentation on some events cannot rule out the existence of a beneficiary, comments such as the following description of a May 22, 1883, theatrical suggest that in the 1880s it was no longer uncommon for amateur theatricals to be staged in public venues simply as entertainment: "At the Lexington Avenue Opera House, the Amateur League gave its seventh dramatic performance and reception of the season. The entertainment was not a complimentary one, but was given for the purpose of establishing a fund for the purchase of a club-room."[53] Countless other advertised or reviewed events are conspicuously lacking a beneficiary. Had it finally become appropriate for middle- and upper-class women to act in public?

Late-century increases in the respectability of theatre could do little to prevent vociferous public outcry over a society woman's choice to leave the amateur stage and work in the commercial theatre. Perhaps one of the most famous defectors was Mrs. Brown Potter, who parlayed her success in the New York amateur theatrical scene into a thirty-year career as a professional performer. As an amateur Brown Potter rarely performed with a titled dramatic group, and her acting and marketing skills enabled her events to become associated with her own name. She took her condoned amateur reputation and the power it provided overseas and began her commercial career in England and then returned to make her professional debut in New York on October 31, 1887, amid much fanfare and scandalous gossip. Her first years as a professional were plagued by contractual issues, a high-profile divorce, charges of ruining the family name, and an eventual love affair and rumored second marriage to her costar, Kryle Bellew. Behaviors and individual public notices that had been passably acceptable in charity theatricals were most decidedly not respectable choices for a woman of her social status. In the eyes of society she had been corrupted by the evils of the world and was no longer able to embody the role of the mythic benevolent female who could help others by remaining unscathed by immorality. Indeed, the outcry's subtext suggested that Mrs. Brown Potter's choice to go pro meant that she was unable to maintain her own moral superiority, thereby proving that she was somehow not a proper woman.

Despite the increased acceptability of theatre, therefore, many of the old stereotypes and preconceptions about the theatrical profession remained throughout the last half of the nineteenth century. Tracy Davis argues that nineteenth-century women existed in a realm where "[s]ocial respectability was merited as long as women met the views prescribed for their age and class, but actresses—virtually by definition— lived and worked beyond the boundaries of propriety."[54] For any woman respectability depended as much on her actual behavior as on the public's perceptions of her behavior, thus rendering the creation of reputations to be, at best, an imprecise process.

It would be easy to assume that amateurs who joined this increasingly respectable profession would naturally end up in the upper echelon of the profession and would maintain their respectability, yet the evidence points to a much more conflicted response and result. Many amateurs were believed to have talent, but they lacked the training and skills necessary to land them in the upper ranks of performers in terms of aesthetic success. Furthermore, parental responses to a daughter's desire to turn professional, daughters' behaviors while making the transition, and the general social and parental responses afterward seem to suggest that the profession, no matter how respectable it might have been for others, was not a viable choice for *their* daughters. Despite the increasing respectability of theatre, the social ostracism, disinheritance, parental wrath, and private detectives who trailed many a society-member-turned-pro suggest that this appearance of respectability and appearance of acceptance was only capable of being maintained from a safe distance. For many, that distance did not involve personal connections with the theatre establishment; indeed, it seems that although many wished to remain in the role of audience, or even adoring fan, that affection did not extend to the idea of making the commercial theatre part of the family.

That distance, however, kept shrinking. Amateur performances were generally held within the bounds of propriety, but those bounds became increasingly porous as the nineteenth century progressed and the already close links between the amateur and the professional stage rendered the two harder and harder to distinguish. Even though some commercial performers were able to shed the immoral stigma that had been previously assumed of most actresses, all was not yet well for the amateurs who wished to turn professional. Yet just as the use of commercial spaces was seen as variably acceptable, so too was the choice to join the profession. For some middle-class women the shifts in public perception of commercial theatre and the popularity of amateur theatricals led to an increasing acceptability of the stage as a professional choice. As Davis notes, "With a different type of play and a different audience, however, the theatre became an attractive career for middle-class women, though the idea of one's daughter exhibiting herself before one's peers was still loathsome to parents."[55] Again, for the amateur this performance before peers was acceptable so long as it was under some means of societal reputation protection; early in the fad the parlor provided this safety. Charity enabled women to maintain their reputations even while performing on commercial stages and eventually doing so alongside professionals. Clubs and dramatic societies also afforded a cover for their public performances, and community theatres that developed after the turn of the century continued the tradition. This trajectory toward activities that were increasingly closer to and modeled on commercial theatre—even as the acceptance of the commercial theatre grew—kept amateur performers so close to the taint of the commercial stage that only their reputations did protect them, at least until they decided to take up the profession.

Despite outcries over actual participation in commercial theatre, the nature of amateur theatricals by the end of the nineteenth century aligns them more closely with commercial theatre than with the parlor entertainments of the 1850s. Amateurs advertised their events; charged admission; used commercial venues; expended great amounts of time, money, and energy in creating aesthetically pleasing entertainments; and interacted with commercial actors by hiring them as coaches or limited engagement stars or by joining commercial shows as supernumeraries. Although all performances did not blend the commercial and amateur, the point remains that this explosion of amateur activity was initially made socially viable because theatricals were staged for charity. What began as groups of women performing their socially appropriate role in public had devolved into thinly veiled opportunities for public displays of self. The once-clear distinctions between amateur and professional theatre were obfuscated by women doing exactly what society wanted them to do. Indeed, a legal case between William Gillette and the Mansfield Amateur Dramatic Association in the early 1890s determined that the presence of paychecks was the only way to legally distinguish between an amateur and a professional.[56] Ethically and morally, the distinction rested entirely on the perceptions of the public.

Notes

1. "Private Theatricals," *New York Times,* July 27, 1855.

2. The terms *private* and *amateur* were used interchangeably to refer to theatricals during the period, and although parlor performances were rarely called "amateur" theatricals, performances in halls and theatres used both names.

3. This is not to suggest that charity events in public theatres in the 1860s did not occur. A particularly novel event was an 1864 charity production of *Cinderella* at Niblo's Garden, staged in part by the children from Mr. Allen Dodworth's dancing academy. The event was described as having "a highly interesting character.... Private theatricals seldom take so pleasant a shape as

this, and we will venture to say that the young folks will be rewarded for their efforts" (Amusements, *New York Times,* April 16, 1864). This afternoon benefit for the Sanitary Commission represented numerous departures from prewar practices, for it was a charity event in a public theatre staged by children. These once-novel practices were followed with regularity in the postwar years, although records of children on the charity stage remain rare.

4. This postwar growth in popularity may be related to the availability of performance spaces, for charitable events that produced large donations necessarily required an audience larger than could fit in even a private ballroom.

5. Rita Lawrence, *Amateurs and Actors of the 19th–20th Centuries (American, English, Italian)* (Plymouth, UK: William Brendon and Son, 1935), 107.

6. "Private Theatricals," *New York Times,* July 27, 1855.

7. Lawrence, *Amateurs and Actors,* 44.

8. G. J. Barker-Benfield, "The Origins of Anglo-American Sensibility," in *Charity, Philanthropy, and Civility in American History,* ed. Lawrence J. Friedman and Mark D. McGarvie (Cambridge, UK: Cambridge University Press, 2003), 87.

9. Ibid., 85.

10. Ibid.

11. Wendy Gamber, "Antebellum Reform: Salvation, Self-Control, and Social Transformation," in *Charity, Philanthropy, and Civility in American History,* ed. Lawrence J. Friedman and Mark D. McGarvie (Cambridge, UK: Cambridge University Press, 2003), 129.

12. Ibid., esp. 129–30.

13. Ibid., 152–53.

14. Lori D. Ginzberg, *Women and the Work of Benevolence: Morality, Politics, and Class in the Nineteenth-Century United States* (New Haven, CT: Yale University Press, 1990), 216.

15. Ibid.

16. There were a few notable amateurs, such as Elsie de Wolfe and Edward Fales Coward, who lent their talents to multiple amateur dramatic societies and thus did operate on what can be viewed as a version of the star system.

17. I have located few records of amateurs ever staging a charity theatrical for the Actor's Fund or any other charity that would have benefited professional actors or any segment of commercial theatre production aside from the occasional benefit performance held for the acting coach with which a particular amateur troupe regularly worked. It appears that the amateurs decided to forgo the chance to further establish their moral superiority over the commercial theatre by working to benefit that morally bereft segment of society. Perhaps they assumed that the actors chose to lower themselves in ways that impoverished youth did not, or perhaps they perceived that their already precarious moral positioning might be weakened by such a clear connection between the two realms of theatre. As always, this hole in the historical record may also be due to the ephemeral nature of amateur performance's historical documentation.

18. For amateurs who chose to adopt a professional career there seemed to be a general consensus among critics that the amateur needed to display innate

talents but that those talents then needed to be shaped and groomed. The amateur tradition of hiring professionals to work on productions as coaches and stage managers can be seen as a means by which a talented amateur could obtain the professional skills necessary to survive on the professional stage.

19. "The Bijou Opera-House," *New York Times,* Sep. 10, 1882.
20. Amusements, *New York Times,* Feb. 25, 1881.
21. "A Russian Honeymoon," *New York Times,* Dec. 30, 1885.
22. "Amateur Performance at the Union League Club," *New York Times,* Feb. 9, 1872.
23. This concern over propriety often accompanies a general dismissal of antitheatrical arguments. Most of the suggested plays are farces or comedies, often translated and offered for sale by the author or publisher, with the occasional domestic drama and fanciful piece for children thrown in for variety. Within this context the contemporary plays that appear most frequently in the guides can be seen as exemplifying the type of theatre that the authors, at least, deemed appropriate. *Caste, Money,* and Robertson's *Home* appear frequently in the texts, although it must be noted that the publishers ran ads for plays that are less obviously part of the commercial shift toward a more gentlemanly melodrama and toward plays otherwise appropriate for middle-class consumption.
24. "Amateurs at the Lyceum," *New York Times,* May 6, 1886.
25. This development of associations parallels the development of women's clubs prior to the 1860s and is part of a larger trend toward participation in events and groupings outside of the home.
26. Kathleen D. McCarthy, "Women and Political Culture," in *Charity, Philanthropy, and Civility in American History,* ed. Lawrence J. Friedman and Mark D. McGarvie (Cambridge, UK: Cambridge University Press, 2003), 182.
27. The social organizations in which women chose to invest their time and energy were, understandably, determined in part by their class and social circles. Ginzberg notes that "conservative benevolent women were far more likely than abolitionists to be members of wealthy, locally influential family and community networks, and their benevolent goals and means reflected the economic and political privileges of their class" (Ginzberg, *Women and the Work of Benevolence,* 6).
28. "Summary of Amusements: Benefit of the New-York Infant Asylum," *New York Times,* March 17, 1872.
29. "Plays by Amateur Actors," *New York Times,* May 17, 1894.
30. Christian Blanchet, "The Universal Appeal of the Statue of Liberty," in *The Statue of Liberty Revisited: Making a Universal Symbol,* ed. Wilton S. Dillon and Neil G. Kotler (Washington, DC: Smithsonian Institution Press, 1994), 31.
31. Barbara A. Babcock and John J. Macaloon, "Everybody's Gal: Women, Boundaries, and Monuments," in *The Statue of Liberty Revisited: Making a Universal Symbol,* ed. Wilton S. Dillon and Neil G. Kotler (Washington, DC: Smithsonian Institution Press, 1994), 84.

32. "Statue of Liberty," *New York Times*, Nov. 15, 1882; "The Beacon of Liberty," *New York Times*, Nov. 26, 1882.

33. "Bartholdi Statue Fund Benefit," *New York Times*, Feb. 4, 1883. For lists of attendees see the former and "In Aid of the Bartholdi Statue," *New York Times*, Jan. 14, 1883; and "The Bartholdi Statue Fund," *New York Times*, Jan. 28, 1883.

34. Charles H. Crandall, *The Season, an Annual Record of Society in New York, Brooklyn, and Vicinity* (New York: White, Stokes, and Allen, 1883), 363–67.

35. Babcock and Macaloon, "Everybody's Gal," 79.

36. From March through September of 1885 Pulitzer took it on himself to regularly post the amount received for the funds, opportunities for donations, and repeated exhortations to support the statue.

37. "National Guard Gossip," *New York Times*, March 29, 1885; "For the Pedestal Fund," *New York Times*, April 14, 1885.

38. The World of Society, *New York Times*, March 29, 1885.

39. For listings of participants and box-holders see "For the Pedestal Fund," *New York Times*, April 13, 1885; The World of Society, *New York Times*, May 3, 1885; and "Helping the Pedestal Fund," *New York Times*, May 9, 1885.

40. Editorial, *New York Times*, Oct. 17, 1885.

41. Ibid.

42. The World of Society, *New York Times*, Sep. 6, 1885.

43. "For the Grant Monument," *New York Times*, Feb. 24, 1886.

44. Ibid.

45. City and Suburban News, *New York Times*, June 8, 1879; Amusements, *New York Times*, May 18, 1870.

46. For a detailed discussion of the twelve-year design and construction process for the Grant Monument see David M. Kahn, "The Grant Monument," *Journal of the Society of Architectural Historians* 41, no. 3 (Oct. 1892): 212–31.

47. "For the Bartholdi Pedestal," *New York Times*, Jan. 3, 1884.

48. "Rebuilding the Standard," *New York Times*, March 27, 1884.

49. "Some Happenings in Good Society," *New York Times*, Dec. 10, 1899.

50. The World of Society, *New York Times*, Feb. 8, 1885.

51. The World of Society, *New York Times*, June 7, 1885.

52. City and Suburban News, *New York Times*, Nov. 17, 1886.

53. Crandall, *The Season*, 394.

54. Tracy C. Davis, *Actresses as Working Women* (London: Routledge, 1991), 3.

55. Ibid., 77.

56. The details of this case can be traced through a series of newspaper articles in the *New York Times* and the *New York Dramatic Mirror*, in particular. Summaries of the case are found in "Gillette and the Amateurs," *New York Times*, July 2, 1891; and "In Favor of Gillette," *New York Dramatic Mirror*, July 11, 1891.

The Doomed Courtesan and Her Moral Reformers

Rachel Rusch

One of the eminent myths in nineteenth-century Western literature has been the story of the doomed courtesan, destined to love truly but damned by a social imperative to perish. The accompanying myth ingrained in the study of this figure is that she is somehow monolithic, as if the heavy role of fate in her story leaves no room for other defining characteristics. In truth the doomed courtesan takes on many forms over the course of the century, as the character is constantly adapted according to the social demands of her era. Authors shaped the role to fit the prevailing morality of their time, using it either as proof or reproof of the society's fears. In this essay I will show the mutual transformations of the doomed courtesan and her moral reformers by tracking the most paradigmatic of these figures—Marguerite Gautier, the lady of the camellias—as she is represented in Alexandre Dumas *fils*'s *La dame aux camélias,* Emile Augier's *Le mariage d'Olympe,* and finally Tennessee Williams's *Camino Real.*

The role of the doomed courtesan found its supreme expression in nineteenth-century France, where countless plays, operas, and novels portrayed women who rose from humble origins to become the mysterious women whose favors might be purchased only by a discriminating clientele with both the taste and the money to appreciate them. These women belonged to the *demimonde,* a term coined by Alexandre Dumas fils to describe a society "which sails like a floating island in the Parisian ocean and which hails, admits, and accepts all who fall, all who emigrate, all who escape from the mainland, not to mention haphazard wrecks of fortune whose original abode is unknown."[1] Dumas fils's formulation placed these women in a half-world. The notion of a "half-world" gives the sense that the residents of this world have somehow been excised from the everyday world of the living and now reside in a liminal space where they are *close* to the real world but not quite *in* it—their floating island. This sort of indistinct existence disturbed many in the bourgeoisie, but there was also the worry that pulling the prostitute back into the definite society in which they themselves dwelt might allow her sins to reenter their comfortable world and contaminate it. Unsure of how to contend with her, dramatists of the nineteenth century pushed the courtesan out of that liminal space and into the certainty of the grave.

The essential example of the *demimondaine* comes, of course, from the author who coined the word. Dumas fils's Marguerite Gautier, heroine of *La dame aux camélias,* is the representation of the doomed courtesan from which all the rest spring. The theatrical version of *La dame aux camélias* was adapted in 1851 by Dumas fils from his own successful novel. The play chronicles the failed love affair of Armand Duval and Marguerite Gautier, Paris's most sought-after courtesan. Her renowned beauty is made all the keener by the promise that it will never fade into age, as Marguerite has the lethal diagnosis of a hereditary form of consumption. Fatality tinges her every breath, giving her splendor a frailty that appeals to the romantic taste for the bittersweet. Armand, smitten from afar, keeps vigil during one of Marguerite's illnesses. The gesture's devotion deeply affects Marguerite when she learns of it, leading her to abandon her practical sensibilities and take Armand as her lover and not her client. As Armand professes, to make a virgin fall in love with you is no great trick, but to win the heart of a woman who has so often sold it is a notable accomplishment indeed. Marguerite somehow believes that she still can possess a virgin heart despite her commercial worldliness and that she and Armand can behave as if they truly were innocent young lovers. The two spend a summer idyll away from Paris and Marguerite's professional demands, but both Marguerite's money and her health have begun to run out when Armand's father arrives and begs Marguerite to give up Armand so as not to thwart the respectable bourgeois marriage of Armand's sister. Marguerite agrees but does not disclose to her lover her true reasons for leaving. She returns to the protection of an old patron while Armand nurses his wounds. The reunion of the lovers and resolution of their differences comes only at Marguerite's deathbed, as she expires in Armand's arms, her passage into the beyond smoothed by his loving words.

Marguerite Gautier's origin was in Dumas' real-life mistress, Marie Duplessis. Duplessis was a famed courtesan, counting among her lovers multiple European nobles and the composer Franz Liszt. Born a peasant girl in Normandy in 1824, Duplessis moved to Paris as part of the widespread urban migration in the 1830s. There she became engaged as a salesgirl in a dress shop; such stores were often simply "pretext shops," fronts for unregistered prostitution that took place away from the government's watchful eye. Soon after coming to Paris, Duplessis taught herself to read, and by the age of sixteen was well versed in both literature and fashionable culture. This appearance of breeding allowed her to reinvent herself as a high-class courtesan, and before she had reached her seventeenth birthday, Duplessis was already working among the most affluent circle of clients in Paris. She and Dumas fils began their affair in the fall of 1844, but it had ended by the summer of 1845. The two did not remain in contact, but word of her death from consumption in 1847 reached the young man while he was traveling with his father.

Dumas fils began working on the novelization of their affair almost immediately. Having already gone from the real girl who had been born in Normandy to the imagined girl she invented for herself and proffered for sale, she had now become the imaginary girl in the lines of a fiction. Her existence now sprang entirely from the mind of her former lover, who recreated her in the image he preferred of her. She was desirable while alive but perfect in death—whatever social danger was inherent in a lower-class woman's sudden access to the power and wealth of "respectable" men was made anodyne by her early demise. The sort of subtle control that may have been exerted by her patrons in her lifetime was made absolute as the only version of her that survived was that conjured on the page by one of these patrons.

Previously undistinguished, and very much in the shadow of his famous father, Dumas fils saw the story of the doomed Marie as an opportunity to make a name for himself in literature. His success in this endeavor was staggering: his novel *La dame aux camélias* was published in 1848 to wild popularity. Readers were rapturous over the sad tale of Armand Duval and Marguerite Gautier, the thinly veiled portraits of the author and his lover, and adaptations of the novel came quickly. Verdi turned it into the opera *La traviata* in 1853, just a year after Dumas fils had staged his own theatrical adaptation of the work at the Théâtre de Vaudeville. Dumas fils's stage version would have appeared even sooner had it not been rejected by the censors three times for its "indecent" subject matter. The reasons for the play's delay and for its eventual performance reveal the ways in which it was bound up in the social and political fabric of its period.

Unrest had swept Europe in 1848, the year of *La dame aux camélias*' publication, and that in France was some of the most acute. Revolution broke out, King Louis-Philippe was forced to flee to London, and a provisional government declared the start of the Second Republic in

France. The disorganization of the liberal government, however, soon brought a conservative backlash, and workers and petit bourgeois who had been united against the king became divided against one another. Louis Napoleon galvanized the rural masses and was elected to the presidency in a sweeping victory in December of that year. When he refused to step down from the post at the end of his term, a coup attempted to oust him but failed. The victorious Louis Napoleon pronounced himself emperor in 1851. The Duc de Morny, Louis Napoleon's censor, finally allowed the stage adaptation of *La dame aux camélias* to be performed in 1852 precisely *because* it was controversial; the hope was that riotous art would draw off some of the heat of discussion from Napoleon III's own acts.

The play premiered to mixed applause and puzzlement but soon grew into a sensation. The controversy that du Morny hoped would ensue did indeed follow, as did the rise of the play to great popularity. A substantial part of both the novel and the play's appeal lay in the story's nearness to life. As the newly famous son of an already famous father, Dumas fils's exploits had already been the subject of gossip, so audiences were well aware of the story's autobiographical nature. Further underscoring the correspondences, the character of Marguerite's associate, Prudence Duvernoy, actually was played by the real-life Prudence. Such a bit of stunt casting surely heightened the voyeuristic pleasure of the audience at being able to peer behind the velvet curtain and see the sexual exploits of one of France's most renowned courtesans and the illegitimate son of one of France's most famous writers.

The parallels between real life and its stage version continue in the circumstances of Marguerite's entry to prostitution and Duplessis's own; Marguerite begins her life in Paris as an embroiderer in a shop—in all likelihood another of the "pretext shops." Her lovers are surprised to hear of her humble origins, but Marguerite expresses a great longing to find some means of reconnection to her origins. After a fight with a jealous Armand, the pragmatic Marguerite attempts to tell him that their love is impossible: "For a moment I built a whole future on your love. I longed for the country. I remembered my childhood—one always has a childhood to remember whatever one may have become since; but it was nothing but a dream."[2] Marguerite expresses the hope that love will allow her to return to the life that she had left behind in the country, which she sees as representative of the authentic and originary. She imagines that the genuine emotion she ascribes to romance will be restorative, a means of resurrecting the unadulterated self she possessed before it became a sold self that could no longer belong entirely to her. Going back to the place of birth would be a renascence, and her reference to her childhood represents a desire to go back, to undo the self that she has become and rebuild a different self.

Although Marguerite does acknowledge in this speech that such an enterprise is but a dream, she is unable to give up on the fantasy, for she does decide to spend the summer in the country with Armand. This romantic dream cannot exist outside of material reality, however, and even a dream must be paid for in cash. To finance her pure moment of love, Marguerite must secretly sell off the possessions that were the fruits of her prostitution. Any version of a new living self can thus only come from the raw material provided by the socially dead self—the exact inverse of the way Marguerite imagines her restoration. The country girl has long since been lost, so for the city *fille* to return to the country is only an idyll, a brief holiday in an imaginary lost paradise. Marguerite and Armand's remove from the city is a displacement designed to sever them from reality and its constituent social ties. In the country, with no social world but one another, the lovers can approach a sort of *folie à deux*, where each offers up an idealized version of the self that is then taken to even loftier realms by the imaginative transformations of the lover. Reality intercedes in the person of M. Duval, however, who persuades Marguerite to cut her ties with Armand. When the couple splits and the nourishing connection is broken, Armand can find other means of sustenance, but Marguerite cannot. Her return from the fantasy of the country brings with it the renewed reality of her death; time had seemed to stop while the couple was on holiday, but the clock begins to tick again as soon as Marguerite leaves, and her consumption quickly worsens. Her resurrection has proved a doomed enterprise.

Marguerite's ghostly quality, intensified now, has been an intrinsic part of her being since the moment that she entered prostitution. It is not only the specter of death that hangs over her as a result of her hereditary consumption but the vision of a dead self, the ghost of what had been a living woman. This is perhaps most evident in Marguerite's association with a character who serves as a dead version of herself. Early in the play Marguerite's compatriot Nanine explains to one of the clients that during one of Marguerite's particularly bad consumptive spells, she had gone to recover at a spa where "there was a young girl about the same age, suffering from the same illness, who was as like her as a twin sister. . . . And the Duke, in his grief, finding Marguerite so like his lost daughter, begged her to receive him and let him love her as a father."[3] The duke has been Marguerite's financial patron, without demanding the sexual element that such patronage usually entails. She is the duke's ghost daughter, and he is her departed father. The emphasis on the twinning of the two women further underscores a sense of natural kinship. Yet as Nanine continues to explain, "Marguerite was not so much like his daughter morally as physically," for she finds herself unable to resist the lure of the attendant glamour in a courtesan's life, even when there is no longer a financial necessity to live in this way. After her return to Paris from the countryside spa, she takes up her old ways again and "the Duke, with only a portion of his happiness, withheld a portion of her income. The result is that Marguerite has fifty thousand franc's worth of debts."[4] For Marguerite to grant the duke the full measure of his happiness, she would have to be truly like his departed daughter, which would mean becoming once again the departed young girl that she herself was. The move from innocence to knowledge is a one-way journey, however, and Marguerite *cannot* become that girl again. Any attempt at a salvation of Marguerite's character that cannot encompass her sexuality is a foolish one. At best, she might be transformed into a sincere lover, but she can never become a sweet young girl.

Despite the salacious subject matter of *La dame aux camélias,* the play does come to an ultimately conservative end, for what it conserves is the idea of the "good girl" as the only living embodiment of womanhood. Bad girls experience living deaths, and their existences are therefore untenable. The real women die; the characters based on them pass out of the work. Dumas' own standards of what sort of deaths can be accommodated onstage are evident in the self-censorship of his adaptation. Perhaps the most striking cut in translating his novel into a play is his failure to include the scene in which Armand exhumes Marguerite's body so that he may say good-bye to her—a far cry from the decorous deathbed scene that he scripts instead. One reason for this change is suggested by Dumas' later declaration that the stage cannot discuss matters as freely as can a book, for "the book speaks in low tones, in a corner . . . [while] the theatre speaks to twelve or fifteen hundred persons in a group and emanates from the public platform and the public square. The painting of truth in public therefore has its limits."[5] Painting the image of a body in which "the eyes were simply two holes, the lips had gone, and the white teeth were clenched" was apparently too brutal a truth to show to an audience.[6] Vice is acceptable, but ugliness is not. The death of the courtesan thus must be de-physicalized—she does not undergo a bodily death in the play; she is simply written out of it. Too strong a focus on her material body would recall its connection to her sexuality—a carnality that would undermine the idealized spiritual version of Marguerite that Dumas is working so hard to maintain.

Dumas' approach to the presentation of delicate material met with great social approval, as it was seen as part of a new moral vein in the drama itself, in which theatre turned to explorations of contemporary life and its social problems. The subject matter of the work was reflective not only of Dumas' own life but of the ascendance of a new style; the rise of realism demanded that drama should arise from the observation of human behavior, from careful attention to the surrounding world. Truth lay in what could be perceived by the senses and thus could best be transmitted through an accurate depiction of what was available to the senses. Dumas' work was one of the preeminent examples of the new realistic drama, depicting the world of the demimonde with frank language and psychologically complex characters.

The emergence of realism on the stage came partly out of a weariness with the themes and style of the Romantics. Such focus on ideals of beauty came to be seen as unrealistic, particularly as Western Europe began to experience widespread political upheaval in the mid-nineteenth century. Dumas fils's work appeared to the theatregoing public in a time when the streets outside the theatre might be filled with protestors or revolutionaries. The social contract was being written and rewritten with shocking frequency by members of the lower classes who agitated for greater rights and members of the middle class who began to move into the power vacuum created by the dwindling supremacy of the aristocracy. This was a particularly potent factor during Dumas' youth, as the bourgeoisie held great influence during the period of constitutional monarchy (1830–48) that followed the downfall of Charles X—itself the result of the king's vast unpopularity with the bourgeoisie. The move to depict realistically the lives and concerns of the bourgeoisie thus amounted to a political act, for it legitimized the increasing importance of this class by inscribing it into literature. Bourgeois lives were worthy of examination, were worthy of art. They had staked their claim as the up-and-coming power of the century.

The ascendant bourgeoisie possessed a zeal for social reform that became grafted onto the earlier rise of public health systems in the major cities, leading to the formulation of prostitution as a social ill. Use of the language of illness and cure linked these ideas to the notion of the prostitute as a spreader of disease. The whore thus lent herself easily as a metaphor for societal sickness. Much of the rhetoric employed came from the studies that had been made by Alexandre Parent-Duchâtelet, a physician who in the late 1820s had turned his attentions to public health issues, namely the spread of cholera and other waterborne illnesses affecting city dwellers. Already consumed by the study of excrescence and waste, Parent-Duchâtelet began to concentrate on an examination of prostitution. The prostitute was considered a "seminal drain," drawing off the excess of sexuality so that it would not taint middle-class women; she was merely another version of the sewer system that helped ensure the health and hygiene of the social body as a whole. Alain Corbin explains:

> The prostitute enables the social body to excrete the excess of seminal fluid that causes her stench and rots her. This indefensible image assimilates a category of women to both the emunctories, which, from the organicist perspective, discharge humors, secretions, and excretions and permit the survival of the social organism—here an early belief of the Church Fathers is revived—and a drain, or sewer. Thus, Dr. Fiaux . . . speaks of the "seminal drain. . . . " The Physiocrats drew parallels between the necessary circulation and flux of air and water and that of products in the economy—this physical exigency should apply as well to the humors of the social organism.[7]

Marguerite's consumption is thus the physical manifestation of her moral illness as a whore. It chokes cleanliness from the body, crowding out air with disease and weakening its bearer to death. More than anything, it is a disease of *blood*, both in the red splotches that mar Marguerite's pristine white handkerchief and in the sense that this is a disease that has been passed down from her mother.

This focus on disease brought with it the concordant belief in cure. Social dramas were inspired by the notion that art was a device for the betterment of humankind and that its methodical application could bring about social improvement. An artist who could diagnose and dissect a social problem was, then, a doctor who could help cure a society's ills. Dumas was pronounced by contemporary critic Emile Deschanel to be "ce moraliste-anatomiste,"[8] an anatomist of morality. Deschanel goes on to say that Dumas created not only the physiology of his characters but also their pathology. To represent the natural world accurately was, according to this scheme, a virtue in itself, regardless of how unvirtuous the behavior depicted may have been. It was an almost utopian vision of art's ability to transfigure even the basest of subjects. Rather than ignoring low themes to focus on more "suitable" depictions, writers would trace out humanity where it otherwise might be obscured by the grime of its surroundings. The writer's project came to resemble that of the reformers' itself: to ennoble the impoverished elements of human life.

As much praise as Dumas garnered for his ability to analyze such a social ill as prostitution, however, the suspicion that he may have been glamorizing it as well was unshakable. The story was a thinly veiled version of his own life after all, and although his later works did grow more acutely moralizing, *La dame aux camélias* remains a testament to a love (or at least an infatuation) that took possession of the young man. And as much as the play's popularity may have found some foundation in the emergence of realism as the preferred theatrical style, or the diversion that the play offered from troublesome political events of the day, the enticement proffered by its titillating aspects could not be underestimated. The sensory seduction that might be effected by the play worried some contemporary critics, who were concerned that the allure granted to high-class prostitution would come to make even ordinary trick-turning seem acceptable. Further concerns arose from the dangerous social possibilities that critics saw in the form of realism itself: one critic, calling himself Jacques Iconoclaste, warned: "Are you not afraid that the Realist, building upon this precedent, will not show us Albertines of the pavement, doing for forty pennies what the other did for forty thousand francs?"[9] Such critics detected a discomforting difference between Marguerite Gautier and earlier prostitute heroines such as Victor Hugo's eponymous Marion Delorme. Marion becomes wretched and rancorous and can be dismissed as a villain by the end of the work, but even though Marguerite is punished in her way, she retains the sympathy of the audience. The moral lesson here is an ambivalent one, as the upright bourgeois father is the blocking character who comes between the young lovers, and the romantic heroine is a whore. While the whore is shown as unable to be reformed, she *is* able to possess a love whose purity surpasses any felt by the more respectable members of her gender. Even the formerly disapproving M. Duval comes to praise Marguerite, sending her a letter to comfort her in her illness: "Your courage and self-denial are worthy of a better future. You shall have it, I promise you. In the meantime, allow me to assure you of my sympathy and of my highest esteem and regard."[10] When the bourgeoisie praises a demimondaine, the supposedly stable social order has gone askew.

The role that Dumas would come to play in his more-didactic later works is instead filled here by his contemporary, Emile Augier, making his own claim for moral superiority. Augier was particularly concerned that any reassessment of power structures could lead to their outright reorganization. He, too, was mistrustful of Marguerite Gautier's popular appeal, but his greatest fear was that there might be a permeability between drama and life, as the prostitute might be able to intermingle with the bourgeoisie without attracting notice. Such trepidation reflected the uncomfortable fact that the very practice of their profession caused the prostitute to be a part of the middle-class world while being simultaneously situated in the demimonde. Even worse was the knowledge that for most women prostitution was not a lifelong occupation, and thus these women slipped between the world of prostitution and that of the ordinary citizen. Moral reformers like Josephine Butler in England or Maria Deraismes in France wanted to see the prostitute's profession as the result of an inborn lapse for which they could then help her compensate. They sought some distinctive trait that set her apart; the thought that prostitution was an act rather than an identity meant that any woman could become a whore and any whore could seem an average woman. With its penchant for categorization and regulation, the French government had relied throughout the nineteenth century on the registration of prostitutes and the policing of licensed brothels as its means of controlling the sex industry. By the end of the century, however, many reformers had begun to decry the government's complicity in prostitution, demanding deregulation and the criminalization of the profession. But whereas the prior system of registration had provided at least some semblance of whom and where the prostitutes were, the end of the containment of the industry had the paradoxical effect of tearing down the regulatory divide between prostitutes and "ordinary" women so that passage into and out of the profession could take place more seamlessly than ever. In fact, many prostitutes went on to marry and have families of their own, which was the greatest affront, in Augier's eyes. The incipient terror was that the whore could infiltrate the bourgeois family and pass herself off as a respectable wife.

Augier wrote *Le mariage d'Olympe* in 1855 as a direct reaction to the popularity of *La dame aux camélias*. In the play he returns real villainy to the prostitute and thus strikes a blow for moral clarity. In *Le mariage d'Olympe* the Parisian courtesan Olympe Taverny has falsely reported her own death and assumed an identity as "Pauline" to marry into a bourgeois family. In fact, "Pauline" is actually Olympe's birth name, so by using it as another level of pseudonymity atop her already famous professional name, she is turning the genuine "Pauline" of her youth into a calculated bastardization of the authentic self—a project that is a perverted version of Marguerite Gautier's own attempt to return to her childhood. Olympe's husband, Henri, is perfectly aware of her true identity but has married her in a paradoxical attempt both to thumb his nose at bourgeois morality *and* to reform the wild Olympe/Pauline to conform to such morality. Augier offers a clear opinion as to how such a confused enterprise could come to pass; in the play's first scene he has Montrichard, the impoverished nobleman, explain to the upright Marquis de Puygiron about the alarming social mobility of prostitutes in the current era:

MONTRICHARD: Do you know that these women have so strong a hold on the public that they have even been made the heroines of plays?
MARQUIS: In the theatre? Women who—? And the audience accepts that?
MONTRICHARD: Without a murmur—which proves that having made their entrée into comedy, they have done likewise into correct society.
MARQUIS: You could knock me down with a feather!
MONTRICHARD: Then what have you to say when I tell you that these ladies manage to get married?
MARQUIS: To captains of industry?
MONTRICHARD: No, indeed—to sons of good families.
MARQUIS: Idiots of good families!
MONTRICHARD: No, no. The bane of our day is the rehabilitation of the lost woman—fallen woman, we say. Our poets, novelists, dramatists, fill the heads of the young generation with romantic ideas about redemption through love, the virginity of the soul, and other paradoxes of transcendental philosophy. These young women must become ladies, grand ladies!
MARQUIS: Grand ladies?
MONTRICHARD: Marriage is their final catch; the fish must be worth the trouble, you see.[11]

Augier is laying the blame for such social confusion squarely at the feet of Alexandre Dumas fils and his fellow dramatists. He believes that the appearance of the courtesan onstage can do the imaginative work of infiltrating the bourgeois mind and, through that, the real-world bourgeois existence.

Dumas and Augier are both considered preeminent authors of the social drama in France, and both are typically lumped together with Scribe as expert practitioners of the well-made play. Such assumptions are deeply mistaken, however, for both the ideology and the structure of Dumas' and Augier's work spring from extremely divergent antecedents. Scribe bequeaths to both writers a devotion to tightly constructed, logical plots that are designed for suspense and speedy movement. Scribe's thin characterizations, however, are weighted and made round by Dumas and are abstracted to a more allegorical schematization by Augier. Dumas' devotion to the principles of realism lead him to invest his characters with nuanced emotions that increase their resemblance to living and breathing people that the audiences could imagine themselves knowing. Although Augier is usually treated as a fellow realist, in truth he eschews a realistic fullness of details in his characters and takes his formal cues from older and more allegorical sources.

It is precisely the dialogue between *La dame aux camélias* and *Le mariage d'Olympe* that reveals the profoundly different literary heritage that each bears. While Dumas is steeped in realism, endeavoring to give his characters plausible psychological motivations, frank speech befitting their characters, and a look behind what transpires in polite society, Augier reaches back to the coffers of melodrama to find stock character types. Geneviève is the good virgin, the marquis the imperious father, Montrichard the libertine, Pauline the temptress. Contemporary critics praised Augier's plotting but often questioned the realism of his characters, suggesting that they behaved according to type rather than to individual psychological motivation. Even the praise offered by critic Gustav Planche, that Augier's characters have "the passions and the foibles that we can find in the grand family of humanity,"[12] offers a telling omission—the characters belong to a general human category but not to a specific place, time, or mentality.

Pauline's husband, Henri, is most overtly a stock type, his qualities based on a preexisting set taken from literature. The play itself enumerates that his character is based on one of Victor Hugo's: Pauline tells Montrichard "Henri took me seriously from the very first. He was most discreet: Didier and Marion Delorme, you see!"[13] This reference to the fictional character from Hugo's 1829 play offers the audience an instant shorthand by which it can categorize Henri's actions and therefore does the work of prejudicing the audience's interpretation of Henri's actions. We know that Henri's belief that he can attempt to reform a renowned courtesan, if only he is strong enough to forgive her many transgressions, is a naive one and doomed to fail. This forceful linking of Augier's play to Hugo's also self-consciously situates the play in its literary context. Dumas had performed a similar function in *La dame aux camélias* when Armand asks Marguerite if she has read *Manon Lescaut,* Abbe Prevost's 1731 novel of a young woman whose taste for luxury and the high life leads her to a series of sexual exploits that denigrates her true emotions for her lover. He chastises Marguerite for the moneymaking scheme he believes her to have: "Marguerite, I know that you have more heart than Manon, and I have more honour than de Grieux."[14] Yet the parallel that Dumas draws ends up flattering his characters, who *do* have more heart and honor than their literary predecessors. Augier, on the other hand, undermines his character by disparaging the earlier character on whose behavior Henri's is based. Augier is not only reacting against the immediate predecessor of Dumas' heroic prostitute but also reaching back farther into the canon to reveal Hugo's reforming gentleman as a fool.

Henri challenges the marquis, accusing him of marrying to defy social convention, saying, "I respect what deserves respect. But the prejudices and absurd conventions, the hypocrisy and tyranny of society—nothing could prevent my despising them as they deserve to be despised!"[15] Yet when Henri is revealed to be a sap, duped by Olympe, his convictions are discredited; the ultimate effect is that opposition to societal convention comes to look naive, and the moral order is reinscribed. Augier rejects Dumas' realism as not morally appropriate and Hugo's romanticism as misleading. It is only in the form of melodrama that he can find the clarity of judgment he seeks to apply in crafting what he terms a comedy of manners—*la comédie de mœurs*. Significantly, Augier shares this word—*mœurs*—with the *police de mœurs*, the agents charged with overseeing the operation of the brothels in nineteenth-century France. The question of "manners" thus contains an overtone of sexual morality, which Augier himself is policing in his drama.

Though Marguerite Gautier herself does not appear in *Le mariage d'Olympe*, her presence pervades the play as a sort of ghost in the machine. She fills the negative space: the entire play exists as a reaction to her, and our antiheroine, Olympe Taverny, is molded to fit exactly what Marguerite is not. Olympe is grasping whereas Marguerite is self-sacrificing; she cracks open the bourgeois family and enters in, where Marguerite walked away to leave it intact; she has a false heart to Marguerite's true one; she is a woman on the ascent while Marguerite is in inexorable decline. She is the evil that M. Duval feared Marguerite was. While Olympe's situation becomes precarious when one of her former lovers recognizes her, she presses ahead with her wicked plans for the family, manipulating her husband's virtuous (and smitten) cousin Geneviève along the way. Just when it seems that Pauline/Olympe's maneuverings will allow her to take both the family's money and its reputation, family patriarch Marquis de Puygiron shoots her dead and proclaims that only God can judge him. Whereas the father in *La dame aux camélias* ended the play remorseful for his exercise of power and humbled to the whore, the one in *Le mariage d'Olympe* can end the play only by establishing the rightness of his dominance, subject to none but the judgment of God.

Through this sort of definition by contradiction, Olympe contains Marguerite, even as she is opposite to her. This reincarnation is strengthened by the fact that at the opening of the play we are told that Olympe Taverny is dead—newspapers have reported that she had absconded to San Francisco, only to perish there. This play thus begins with the death of the whore, just as Dumas' play had ended with it. In this way the torch is passed between the two plays, and Olympe picks up the thread of Marguerite's life. Yet the first (pretended) version we get of Olympe's death is only a metaphoric one—the role of the whore dies, but the woman who performed her does not. Olympe Taverny dies in California that Pauline may be born in Paris. This ability to trade roles back and forth between housewife and courtesan, as well as the pretended move to San Francisco, cannot help but recall the real world exploits of Lola Montez, an Irish teenaged bride who in 1843 split from her husband and refashioned herself as a Spanish exotic dancer. Montez became famous for her sultry stage performances, as well as for her affairs with King Ludwig I of Bavaria, Franz Liszt (who had also been Marie Duplessis's lover), and even Alexandre Dumas *père*. In 1853, just two years before Augier's play, Montez had moved to San Francisco to marry some "ordinary" American. The choice of San Francisco for Olympe's death and resurrection is also thematically significant because the California Gold Rush was but six years old at the time of the play, and the drive westward had allowed vast numbers of people to strike out for new territories and begin new lives, reinventing themselves on the frontier. The implications of gold-digging are also resonant, for Olympe's imaginary gold rush serves only to conceal Pauline's real one.

That Pauline is actually alive stands as an indictment of Marguerite Gautier, for the notion of the courtesan's noble expiration is shown to be not a tragedy but a cheap fake. By extension it is also, of course, an indictment of Dumas fils as a dramatist, as Dumas' supposed realism is treated here as nothing but sentimental fantasy. Augier's allusion to Lola Montez may have been a pointed one as well, as it serves to recall the questionable sexual behavior of Dumas fils's own father. What we come to see by the end of Augier's play is that it is only the violent application of bourgeois morality that can accomplish the bona fide death of the whore. The marquis's action closes the chapter not only on Marguerite as a character but on the entire genre of the prostitute heroine that she represented. Augier thus kills Marguerite once so that Olympe can be grotesquely formed out of her ashes and then a second time as he blasts her from the earth. Even death cannot be trusted when coming from a whore; she cannot enact her own end but must be exterminated by the righteous bourgeoisie. The body of the whore must expire *and* her spirit must be exorcised.

Augier's bid for moral clarity came at the start of a new era of thinking about female representation in France. In 1869 feminist reformer Maria Deraismes founded the Association for the Rights of Women, which sought to improve the conditions and educational opportunities for women. In her writings Deraismes called for a new conception of women in the public eye; she wrote that in the theatre "man composes woman according to prejudices and his passions, and that woman, in turn, models herself upon this fantastic creation."[16] In this formulation even a real woman becomes a character restricted by the genre in which she is conceived, as she adopts the artificial conduct scripted by the dramatist as her own behavior in her real life. While Augier was worried that men would be seduced by the idea of the noble courtesan, Deraismes worried that *women* would be seduced by the idea because of its very hold on the male imagination.

The favor granted to the genre of courtesan literature helped to galvanize the reformers into making real-world changes in social policy that served to stamp out the very inspiration for these dramatic works. Drama, accordingly, shifted its focus from the preternatural tragic beauty of the prostitute to her very real-world social situation. The end of the nineteenth century in France saw the closing of many brothels and a movement toward the decentralized (and decidedly down-market) world of wine-shop prostitution, or simple streetwalking. The gilded veneer was wearing off, and although the trade of prostitution itself thrived, as ever, its more glamorous trappings had fallen from favor. The pretty and doomed Marguerite Gautier of literature gave way to the grotesquerie of Zola's Nana, her own sickness not a picturesque consumption but a revolting assemblage of blisters and sores. The realism of Dumas' depiction of a social milieu was replaced by Zola's naturalism, which took as its aim the most complete scientific and medical description of even the most disgusting aspects of natural life. The prostitute in literature had ceased to be the doomed courtesan and had become the damned whore.

The figure of Marguerite Gautier was thus largely retired from the authorial imagination for several decades, her memory tended by the stage actresses who remained devoted to playing the role of Camille. When Marguerite is once again recreated by the pen in Tennessee Williams's *Camino Real*, she is a changed creature, and the drama is a changed form. Williams's 1953 play is a highly theatricalist work, exposing the mechanics of theatre itself as it depicts a carnival of lost souls adrift on the Camino Real—both the Royal Road and the Real. Many of the principals in Williams's drama are refugees from other literary works—Don Quixote and Sancho Panza appear, as do Jacques Casanova and our own Marguerite Gautier. In the plaza of some seedy port town they mix with the mythic World War II American soldier Kilroy, a lordly man named Gutman, loan sharks, mummers, vendors, and a gypsy whose daughter's virginity is magically restored and resold with each new moon. This is a place where "the spring of humanity has gone dry,"[17] and Don Quixote seeks someone to help him escape to a more hopeful horizon, but the only way out appears to be on a plane called the *Fugitivo*, which no one seems able to catch.

Marguerite is holed up here in a hotel with her lover, the legendary Jacques Casanova. She still has her furs and jewels, and trails her old servants Prudence and Olympe behind her, but otherwise she seems to have left her old life. Unwelcome reminders of it arrive on a silver platter, however, as a waiter delivers a letter containing a brochure for the Bide-a-While resort—ostensibly a mountain retreat but really a sanatorium for consumptives. Marguerite tells Jacques about the place: "I wasn't released. I left without permission. They sent this to remind me."[18] She has died but has refused to die, and thus death keeps trying to come to reclaim her. On one level Marguerite's statement serves to remind both audience and lover of her corrosive sickness. But on another level this alerts us that what this Marguerite has left without permission is the confines not only of the hospital but of the drama that housed her. The letters that the Bide-a-While sends Marguerite are almost like missives from the nineteenth century being sent into the heart of the twentieth century, infiltrating it, forcing the drama of the twentieth century to incubate and sustain the stories of the nineteenth.

Marguerite is an escapee from Dumas' play, no longer subject to the rules of the dramatic world that had contained her. She has cheated death by breaking free from the fatal sentence of *La dame aux camélias*, but the price paid for death is time. Dumas kept her eternally young, her beauty frozen by the stopping of the clock. But this Marguerite is subject to age and loss and disillusionment. She tells Jacques of how she used to place a white camellia outside her door every day but for the five each month when it was pink—a notice to her lovers that the great courtesan was indisposed for the week. She says that now the camellia is always white, meaning that what we have now is a post-menopausal Marguerite. That the paragon of youthful efflorescence should undergo any kind of sexual withering is a shock. But whereas Dumas could not allow a prostitute to bear a pure love in a sullied life, and so snuffed out that life, Williams suggests that there is a whole existence to be lived after the time of the initial ardor. There is a reckoning that comes not from the pressure of outside social forces but from within, as one must contend with what Marguerite calls "the sort of desperation that comes after even desperation has been worn out through long wear!"[19]

This loss of even the idea of innocence is the marker of *Camino Real*'s position as a drama of the twentieth century rather than the nineteenth. Williams's work entered a cultural landscape vastly different from that in which *La dame aux camélias* found its reception. In the 1850s France was entering a time of great decadence, and the bourgeois objections to Marguerite and her milieu were against the frank depictions of the sexuality being practiced in contemporary society. In the 1950s the anxiety is not about the ability of the Other to assimilate into society but about the possibility that there is an Other that never will, that will stand in refusal of bourgeois morality. Significantly, the contemporary objections to Williams's drama were not about the sexual subject matter but the political: Walter Winchell and Ed Sullivan both attacked *Camino Real* as an anti-American, leftist manifesto.[20] The play's setting in a sort of surreal Latin American police state was meant to serve as an antifascist commentary, but to critics it smacked of communism. Esmeralda's benediction, "God bless all con men and hustlers and pitchmen who hawk their hearts on the street,"[21] reproached the conformity of 1950s society in America. Marguerite, "the courtesan who made the mistake of love,"[22] is but one of a troupe of the rejected and cast out. The moral reformers cannot hold sway over this Marguerite, for the bourgeoisie has met its own breakdown as even the quintessential brave American soldier, Kilroy, is but another one of the misfits on the Camino. The monolith has broken down as morality no longer seems so fixed, and even dramatic form begins to implode as Williams mixes carnival, pageant, farce, romance, satire, tragedy, and comedy.[23] What Williams offers is neither realism nor melodrama but a modern version of romance, the restoration of a sick world and the promise of continued life. Marguerite laments to Jacques that "tenderness, the violets in the mountains—can't break the rocks!"[24] But as the dry fountain in the plaza begins to flow and a reconciled Marguerite takes Jacques's hand, Don Quixote announces, "The violets in the mountain have broken the rocks!"[25] This is a different kind of redemption from the one imagined by the doomed courtesan's moral reformers but one that seems more real. The doomed courtesan may not get a happy ending, but she does get one that contains a glimmer of hope.

Notes

1. Alexandre Dumas fils, *Le demi-monde*, 2.8.
2. Alexandre Dumas, *Camille*, in *"Camille" and Other Plays*, ed. Stephen S. Stanton (New York: Hill and Wang, 1957), 133.
3. Ibid., 108.
4. Ibid., 109.
5. Alexandre Dumas fils, preface to *Étrangère*.
6. Alexandre Dumas fils, *La dame aux camélias*, trans. David Coward (Oxford: Oxford University Press, 1986), 38.
7. Alain Corbin, "Commercial Sexuality in Nineteenth-Century France," in *The Making of the Modern Body*, ed. Catherine Gallagher and Thomas Laqueur (Berkeley: University of California Press, 1987), 210–11.

8. Bernard Weinberg, "Contemporary Criticism of the Plays of Dumas Fils, 1852–1869," *Modern Philology* 37, no. 3 (Feb. 1940): 297.

9. Ibid., 301.

10. Emile Augier, *Olympe's Marriage*, in *"Camille" and Other Plays*, 160–61.

11. Ibid., 169.

12. Bernard Weinberg, "Contemporary Criticism of Emile Augier, 1845–1870," *Modern Philology* 36, no. 2 (Nov. 1938): 185 (my translation).

13. Augier, *Olympe's Marriage*, 177.

14. Dumas, *Camille*, 125.

15. Augier, *Olympe's Marriage*, 181.

16. Quoted in Amy Millstone, "French Feminist Theater and the Subject of Prostitution, 1870–1914," in *The Image of the Prostitute in Modern Literature*, ed. Pierre L. Horn and Mary Beth Pringle (New York: Ungar, 1984), 20.

17. Tennessee Williams, *Camino Real*, in *The Theatre of Tennessee Williams*, vol. 2 (New York: New Directions, 1971), 435.

18. Ibid., 498.

19. Ibid., 502.

20. Donald Spoto, *The Kindness of Strangers: The Life of Tennessee Williams* (Boston: Little, Brown, 1985), 187.

21. Williams, *Camino Real*, 585.

22. Ibid.

23. Jan Balakian, "Williams's Allegory about the Fifties," in *The Cambridge Companion to Tennessee Williams*, ed. Matthew C. Roundané (Cambridge, UK: Cambridge University Press, 1997), 69.

24. Williams, *Camino Real*, 527.

25. Ibid., 591.

Gender and (Im)morality in Restoration Comedy

Aphra Behn's *The Feigned Courtesans*

Leah Lowe

RECENT CRITICAL ANALYSES of the comedies of Aphra Behn (1640–89), often guided by interpretive strategies designed to illuminate differences between Behn and her male contemporaries, reveal interesting tensions between her female characters and the roles they play in the male-dominated narratives in which they appear. Composed for the notoriously sexual Restoration stage, Behn's plays deal with licentious rakes and knowing women embroiled in narratives thick with intrigue. As a female playwright in a competitive marketplace, Behn drew on theatrical models that were successful, including that of the marriage-plot comedy that first challenges conventional morality through its celebration of sexual license and then reconciles itself to social mores through a predictable conclusion in which "the beautiful people are married with the blessing of the guardians."[1] Like those of her male peers, Behn's comedies featured rakish heroes intent on sexual conquest and gratification regardless of social consequences. At the same time, Behn created active female characters who display wit, intelligence, and sexual desire of their own, throwing into sharp relief the different social standards by which male and female sexual behaviors were judged. Behn's female characters, while of their own particular historical moment and subject to its significant restrictions, trouble the sexual politics of the worlds they inhabit by demonstrating a sexuality that is responsive to their own desire, as well as to the strict social constraints that bind it.

A reading of Behn's *The Feigned Courtesans; or, A Night's Intrigue* (1679) offers ample opportunity to explore Behn's representations of gender differences in relationship to prevailing moral codes within the generic outlines of the Restoration marriage-plot comedy. The main plot follows the adventures of two attractive aristocratic Italian sisters, Marcella and Cornelia, as they outwit their aged guardian, Count Morosini, and escape an arranged marriage (in Marcella's case) and a celibate life in a convent (in Cornelia's). The socially respectable and chaste young women run away to Rome, where they disguise themselves as courtesans and pursue, and are ultimately betrothed to, two dashing young British cavaliers of their own choice. Marcella, the more socially conventional and romantic of the two, disguises herself as the courtesan Euphemia to pursue the equally conventional Fillamour. Her witty sister, Cornelia (who poses as La Silvianetta), is after his rakish friend, Galliard. Fillamour and Galliard, confused by the women's disguises, also pursue Marcella/Euphemia and Cornelia/Silvianetta respectively, though in different ways with different goals in mind. An important secondary plot focuses on a third rich and beautiful virgin, Laura Lucretia, who also disguises herself as a courtesan and also adopts the name La Silvianetta in order to avoid an arranged marriage and win Galliard's love, further complicating the elaborately tangled confusion of identity that characterizes the play's action. In the end Count Morosini and Octavio, Marcella's fiancé, relent and withdraw their objections to the unions of Marcella and Cornelia with their respective cavaliers. Though the play is ultimately resolved by the unions typical of romantic comedy and both Marcella and Cornelia are promised to the appropriate cavalier, Laura Lucretia does not win the man of her dreams, inserting an ambivalent note in an otherwise typical happy ending.

Marriage-plot or romantic comedy, structured around the development of a heterosexual union (or, in the case of *The Feigned Courtesans,* three of them), tends to follow a familiar three-part narrative pattern. Northrop Frye observes that an initial oppressive situation is altered through the course of a topsy-turvy phase of the story in which identities are often disguised, social statuses reversed, rules broken, and social standards challenged. The typical romantic comedy is ultimately resolved, Frye argues, through the establishment of a transformed society, usually symbolized by a marriage, in which social control passes from the father or paternal figure to the son, who, finally united with a female partner, is ready to create a new family.[2] Female characters often play crucial roles in romantic comedies. Because they are generally of lower social status in the patriarchal worlds they inhabit, their prominence through the middle phase of the comedy marks the temporary suspension of ordinary social rules and customs, though the nature of that suspension and the ordinary rules that are set aside vary across specific comedies. As willing brides at the end of various romantic comedies, female characters contribute to the sense that the particular social worlds of their narratives have been righted.

The romantic comedy's disorderly middle phase has long fascinated critics because it elevates members of its social world that are generally recognized as powerless and flaunts, for a finite span of time, values that ordinarily are espoused by the society it represents. Film scholar Kathleen Rowe describes this middle phase as a narrative space within the comedy "marked by what Bakhtin would call the carnivalesque, Victor Turner the liminal, and Frye and C. L. Barber a 'green world' of festivity and renewal set apart from the 'red and white' world of politics and history."[3] Tensions between the transgressive middle phase of marriage-plot comedy, which I, borrowing the terminology of anthropologist Victor Turner, will call "liminal,"[4] and its comparatively stable conclusion give rise to debate about whether this type of comedy is an inherently conservative form that reinscribes traditional attitudes and social structures or one that, through its inversions and reversals, enables new ways of thinking about the values of the society it represents. In the broader context of a discussion of romantic comedy as a dramatic form concerned with both feminine agency and social order, *The Feigned Courtesans* invites consideration of what its liminal representations of femininity, constructed through opposition to patriarchal regulation, do and do not accomplish in an ideological sense.

As *The Feigned Courtesans* begins, each of its heroines is denied the marriage partner of her choice by a paternal authority figure. In the play's liminal phase each woman takes her future into her own hands as she leaves home and assumes the identity of a glamorous courtesan in order to pursue the man she loves. The conclusion of Behn's play represents a generational progression as its heroines and heroes form partnerships that ensure their places in and imply the continuity of the social order, but this generational shift is not accompanied by any significant moral shift within the social order itself. Jane Spencer reads *The Feigned Courtesans* as "an attempt to inscribe female desire within a patriarchal text" and suggests that "in our reading of it, we need to give weight both to the attempt and to its inevitable limitations."[5] Elin Diamond arrives at a similar conclusion when she describes "the interplay of disguise and desire" within the play as "a concentrated and contradictory demonstration of the impossibility of female desire in a phallic economy."[6] Both summations are accurate and provide a solid foundation for further readings of Behn's text. With Spencer and Diamond I will argue that the play upholds the values of its patriarchal social system but is marked by internal contradiction and ambivalence with regard to feminine agency and desire. In contrast to their analyses, my interest in the narrative mechanics of romantic comedy leads me to examine the differences in social acceptability between the feminine and masculine desires expressed in the play and the degree to which its femininities, represented through the characters of Marcella, Cornelia, and Laura Lucretia, first violate social norms and then shift as liminal disguises are abandoned and the play concludes. I do so in order to explore the extent to which autonomous feminine desire can be incorporated in this patriarchal text and what finally resists representation within its conventions. This analytical tack facilitates consideration of the ambivalent relationship between this particular comic narrative and the values of the social order it ultimately endorses, as well as reflection on the dynamics of romantic comedy as a generic form.

Although donning the courtesan's mask grants the three virgins of *The Feigned Courtesans* a temporary freedom of movement, they do not use their disguises in the same way or play their assumed roles to the same effect. Marcella, the older of the two sisters, is troubled by the social implications of her disguise. In her first scene she confesses that the very word *courtesan* startles her.[7] Whereas Cornelia embraces the use of disguise as a tool to pursue her goals, Marcella is concerned about her reputation. She cautions her sister, "A too forward maid, Cornelia, hurts her own fame, and that of all her sex," and reminds her of the importance of others' opinions, observing that there are "charms in wealth and honor" obtained through socially sanctioned marriage (2.1.53–54, 62). Marcella's concern with honor continues throughout the play, but it is important to note that whatever moral qualms she may have about her liminal disguise, it enables her to pursue Fillamour and avoid a forced marriage to Octavio, who is demonized by his description in the cast list as "deformed, revengeful" (90). Cornelia sums up Marcella's liminal strategy when she observes, "[A] little impertinent honor we may chance to lose, 'tis true; but our right-down honesty, I perceive you are resolved we shall maintain" (2.1.77–79). The courtesan mask and the sexual power it grants her, though distasteful to Marcella, allow her to seek her own interests.

Fillamour, her beloved, shares Marcella's concern with honor and reputation, particularly as they apply to the behavior of women. In contrast to his pleasure-loving companion, Galliard, prostitution and the women who practice it disgust Fillamour. While Galliard praises feminine beauty and sexual allure, Fillamour extols virtue, constancy, and lawful marriage. In fact, for Fillamour masculine as well as feminine honor depends on women's virtue. When Julio, Marcella's brother, is informed that his sister has left home with an unknown man, he is outraged and tells his friend Fillamour that his sister and her lover have disgraced her family. Fillamour, equally outraged, asks, "And lives the villain that durst affront ye thus?" and promises, "In all your quarrels, I must join my sword," never imagining that Julio is misinformed and that he, Fillamour, is the villain whom Julio pursues (3.1.85, 94). Although this is a relatively minor incident in the play's tangled plot, it underscores the powerlessness of the kind of femininity Fillamour admires and indicates that the integrity of the patriarchal order demands a feminine sexuality that plays by its rules. Autonomous feminine desire defies paternal control and has the potential to disrupt the social hierarchy maintained by socially sanctioned marriages. Fillamour's ideal woman is one who adheres to social convention and is both chaste and inactive, responding to the desires of paternal authorities rather than acting on any desires of her own. Ironically, it is only Marcella's liminal activity, condemned unknowingly by Fillamour in his defense of Julio's honor and more directly by his disapproval of Euphemia's sexuality, that allows the separated couple to reunite.

In the Marcella-Fillamour love plot it is Marcella who initiates and drives the action. The Marcella-Fillamour plot is full of confusion on Fillamour's part, regarding Marcella/Euphemia's identity. Fillamour oscillates between worshipful idealization of the Marcella whom he loved and sexual attraction to the beautiful, but morally repugnant, Euphemia. Early in the play Galliard, thoroughly smitten with Silvianetta/Cornelia, persuades Fillamour to accompany him on a walk to catch a glimpse of the courtesans. On seeing Euphemia, Fillamour seems to have penetrated her disguise and believes that he has actually seen Marcella. When Galliard insists that the woman is only "a fine, desirable, expensive whore" (2.1.244), Fillamour muses:

> No, no, it cannot, must not be, Marcella.
> She has too much divinity about her,
> Not to defend her from all imputation;
> Scandal would die to hear her name pronounced. (2.1.260–63)

Fillamour's love for Marcella is elevated, spiritualized, and desexualized; he abhors the blatant sexuality and crass economic concerns of the prostitute. Fillamour is the male character who best articulates society's ideal standards for feminine behavior, and his perspective continually reproduces the goddess/whore opposition. Though Marcella is his female counterpart, the woman who most clearly aspires to the same ideal standards of feminine behavior, she is unable to conform to them and pursue her own happiness at the same time. Any degree of social power that she demonstrates is necessarily an infraction of ideal feminine standards.

Throughout the play's liminal phase, interactions between Marcella and Fillamour are marked by a tension between Marcella's activity, which is linked with feminine sexual transgression, and Fillamour's idealization of Marcella, which demands passivity. Marcella routinely misses crucial bits of information that would convince her of Fillamour's love for her and his commitment to honorable sexual standards. To test him, or perhaps to punish him, she continues to perform the role of the courtesan. In act 4, scene 1 she appears to him in La Silvianetta's private rooms, "richly and loosely dressed," according to the play's stage directions (141). The visual aspect of Marcella clad in the courtesan's robes, powerful enough to incite a considerable conflict between Fillamour's desire for her and his principles, provides an ironic counterpoint to the conventional sexual morality both characters espouse. Marcella, ostensibly virtuous, represents herself as a highly sexual creature; and Fillamour, who idealizes feminine virtue, is forced to acknowledge her sexual power. Though Fillamour ultimately rejects Euphemia's advances and lectures her about the social security afforded women by lawful marriage, Behn's theatrical representation of the couple's interactions forces the recognition of a highly charged subtext and emphasizes the sexual dimension of their love.

Although Marcella's courtesan disguise affirms feminine desire and enables her to exercise a degree of social power, this power is curtailed and complicated by the performance context in which she appears on the stage. In a discussion of theatrical conventions in Restoration comedy Elin Diamond notes that "displayed at a distance, the actress in undress becomes a fetish object, pleasuring the male spectator while protecting him from the anxiety of sexual difference."[8] Laura Rosenthal observes:

> Female desire and women's insistence on sexual self-determination shape the conflicts in many Restoration plays; at the same time, the novelty of the female body as a specular and frequently disempowered object contradicted and circumscribed this subjectivity. The dominant, although not the only, subject/object division that emerges constitutes an attempt to secure the social position of women and ensure the domestic authority of men through a sexual objectification of the figure onstage (in her capacity as a performer and character) that conflicts with the character's assertions of sexual subjectivity.[9]

Although Marcella is the play's designated good girl and never really risks her honor, the only way she can exercise power, will, and agency is through manipulation of her social status as a sexual commodity. While her liminal disguise enables her to pursue her own desires by granting her sexual power, this potentially disruptive power is defused by theatrical conventions in which her body is displayed for the titillation of the male spectator.

Jane Spencer observes that tensions between feminine autonomy and sexual objectification are further amplified by the prologue of *The Feigned Courtesans,* originally performed by Betty Currer, who played the role of Marcella.[10] Restoration-era actresses, many of whom retired from the stage to become the mistresses of powerful men, were already associated with prostitution by their audiences, who displayed a "lively, even obsessive concern" with their offstage sexual affairs. Katherine Maus asserts that prologues "with their ambiguous position between the fictional and the real, provided ideal opportunities to exploit the relation between the player and the part."[11] In the prologue Currer refers to the Popish Plot of 1678, a political controversy that resulted in a dramatic decrease in theatre attendance during the 1678–79 season.[12] Currer wittily points out that the sparse audiences have resulted in a personal crisis for her: "Who says this age a reformation wants / When Betty Currer's lovers all turn to saints?" (93). In her reading of the play's prologue Spencer observes, "In the perception of the original audience, the feigned courtesan was being played by a real one, and surely this twists any moral about female truth and honor that the play might express."[13] Currer goes on to complain that because she lacks the financial support of a lover, her clothing has grown worn (94). Not only does Behn's prologue ironically undercut Marcella's virtuous character, but it also sets up the notion of feminine sexuality as a commodity traded for economic security.

If Marcella dons her courtesan garb reluctantly, Cornelia dresses up enthusiastically. Like Marcella, Cornelia intends to keep her virginity, and thus preserve her value on the marriage market, but unlike Marcella, she finds life as a courtesan and its attendant intrigues exciting. She calls it "a glorious profession" and tells Marcella, "Why 'tis a noble title, and has more votaries than religion; there's no merchandise like ours, that of love, my sister" (2.1.69–70). Cornelia enjoys the attention of men, particularly that of her beloved Galliard, and confesses her attraction: "I find enough to do to defend my heart against some of those members that nightly serenade us and daily show themselves before our window" (2.1.80–82). Whereas Marcella flees an arranged marriage, at the end of the play Cornelia admits sexual curiosity when she confesses that she left the convent in order to find a lover (5.4.143). In contrast to Marcella Cornelia recognizes that she is a sexual commodity and is quite matter-of-fact about using her desirability to "catch" Galliard. Cornelia does not assign the same degree of moral value to social opinion and chastity that Marcella does, although she recognizes the crucial importance of marriage as a means of uniting with her beloved without incurring social condemnation.

While Cornelia plays the "antiromantic" to Marcella's "romantic," Galliard's rakishness is set against Fillamour's high-minded virtue.[14] Fillamour extols feminine modesty and honesty, but Galliard wants passion, sex, and love without the restrictions of matrimony. When Fillamour suggests that "lawful enjoyment" of women might offer pleasure (1.1.55), Galliard responds, "Prithee, what's lawful enjoyment but to enjoy 'em according to the generous, indulgent law of nature; enjoy 'em as we do meat, drink, air, light, and all the rest of her common blessings?" (1.1.57–60). For Galliard male sexuality and desire are simply "natural" and unproblematic. He knows no shame in visiting prostitutes or taking mistresses. Constancy does not interest him; he tells the sisters' servant, Petro, that "a new day ought to bring a new conquest" (1.1.172). Galliard's masculine sexuality, however, exists at the expense of women and their inclusion in the play's social order. In contrast to the play's women, for whom marriage is a social necessity, Galliard, who refers to a wife as "a dead commodity," sees marriage as an unpleasant restriction to his personal freedom (4.1.315).

Though Galliard's attitude toward women is decidedly cavalier, he is not entirely without his own principles, inverted with regard to social conventions though they be. In act 4, scene 2, after Cornelia has invited him to her apartment in the dead of night only to explain that she is not actually a courtesan and extract a promise of marriage from him, he is both shocked and offended:

No courtesan! Hast thou deceived me then?
Tell me thou wicked-honest cozening beauty!
Why didst thou draw me in with such a fair pretence,
Why such a tempting preface to invite,
And the whole piece so useless and unedifying?
Heavens! Not a courtesan! (4.2.169–74)

While Galliard's outrage comically inverts conventional morality, it also highlights the differences between socially acceptable masculine and feminine sexualities. Cornelia's desire must be satisfied within the socially sanctioned bonds of marriage or result in social exclusion. Galliard, however, is free to enjoy sex, avoid marriage, and suffer no serious social consequences. Even Fillamour treats Galliard indulgently, disapproving of his sexual excess as a parent might disapprove of a naughty but charming child.

The reformation and inclusion of the rake in the social structure of act 5 is a recurring trope for social cohesion and transformation in Restoration comedy. In *The Restoration Rake-Hero* Harold Weber observes that the Restoration rake is characterized primarily by his sexuality, and Galliard is no exception. Weber observes: "The rake necessarily raises ambivalent responses, for the sexual energy that he represents threatens the stability of the social order even while it promises to provide the vitality that must animate the structures of that order." Weber argues that the rake's rebellious sexuality, ultimately reconciled to the social order through the customary fifth-act marriage that transforms him from a "wanton lover into a satisfied husband," enables the Restoration comedy to demonstrate that masculine individuality can function successfully within the restrictions of society.[15] The witty virgin, in this case Cornelia, plays an important dramaturgical function in the rake's reformation. She becomes the link between the rake, with his "natural" and unlimited sexual appetite, and the social order at which he scoffs.

At the end of *The Feigned Courtesans* an interesting tension develops between the character of Cornelia and the conventional dramaturgical function she plays as she transforms Galliard into a reluctantly good citizen through marriage. Cornelia, witty and actively desiring, has pursued her own pleasure and goals throughout the play. Yet when Galliard, faced with the inevitability of marriage, asks, "Have I been dreaming all this night of a new-gotten mistress, to wake and find myself noosed to a dull wife in the morning?" (5.4.147–49), Cornelia quickly swears to become "the most mistress-like wife," offering him sexual satisfaction as payment for the restrictions of marriage. Though she teases him by declaring that she will be "expensive, insolent, vain, extravagant and inconstant," the sexual power she has enjoyed throughout the play's liminal phase becomes the means of keeping Galliard happy (5.4.154–56). While Galliard is reformed and Cornelia finds a husband, the conventional Restoration trope of the tamed rake results in another ambivalent representation of feminine sexuality, analogous to that of Marcella, as Cornelia's liminal desire and autonomy are not renounced but resituated in relation to Galliard's masculine sexual pleasure.

In the case of the play's third woman, Laura Lucretia, the consequences of overstepping the bounds of socially compliant female sexuality are made clear. Though Laura's subplot is subordinated to those involving Marcella and Cornelia, it is the least formulaic and the strangest of the three. As *The Feigned Courtesans* opens, Laura is pursued by Julio, to whom she is promised in marriage although she has never met him. Laura tells her servant to tell Julio that she is La Silvianetta to put him off the track while she pursues Galliard, with whom she has fallen in love. The notion of love as adventure, as intrigue, and as a high-stakes game between men and women is set up in the play's first few lines as Laura declares, "I must find some way to let [Galliard] know my passion, which is too high for souls like mine to hide" (1.1.11–13). As the play progresses, Laura pursues Galliard in two disguises. She becomes his friend disguised as a man, Count Sans Coeur. She also rents the house next to the house of Marcella and Cornelia and disguises herself as La Silvianetta, creating numerous possibilities for confusion of identity as various characters enter the wrong house in the dark of night.

Throughout the play's liminal phase Laura is the most sexually daring of the play's women. She displays an enthusiasm for the pursuit of love and sexual pleasure that resembles Galliard's, and she is repeatedly associated with masculinity in ways that the play's other women are not. In the play's earliest description of her Laura is referred to as "a brave, masculine lady," and later her success in cross-dressing and impersonating a man is clearly established (1.1.99). Though all the play's women cross-dress at some point during the play's liminal phase, Laura is the only one who does so repeatedly. She is also the only female character who develops a persona and friendships while disguised as a man. Like Galliard, Laura valorizes sexual pleasure and expresses contempt for the social conventions that govern sexual behavior. Echoing Galliard's views on marriage, she describes a wife as an "unconcerned domestic necessary / Who rarely brings a heart or takes it" (2.1.171–72). In contrast to Marcella and Cornelia, Laura refuses to accept the connections between social inclusion, feminine chastity, and marriage. In her pursuit of Galliard Laura repeatedly places love before honor.

Not only is Laura's sexual desire and contempt for conventional morality more closely associated with masculinity than femininity within the play's social context, but her sexuality is further complicated by hints of homoeroticism as she represents herself as Count San Coeur. After making Galliard's acquaintance in her disguise, she confides in her servant:

Ah, Silvio, when he took me in his arms,
Pressing my willing bosom to his breast,

> Kissing my cheek, calling me lovely youth,
> And wondering how such beauty and bravery
> Met in a man so young! (3.1.103–7)

A few moments later, still disguised as a man, she describes her imagined mistress to Galliard:

> My love has a nice appetite,
> And must be fed with high uncommon delicates.
> I have a mistress, sir, of quality. (3.1.123–25).

Though homoeroticism is only suggested, these statements highlight the violation of heterosexual social norms occasioned by Laura's male disguise. A hint of incest arises in act 5, scene 2 when Laura, dressed as a courtesan, greets Galliard, with whom she intends to have sex, as the ghost of her departed brother in order to confuse the other characters present (5.2.56–57). Laura's sexual desire is not merely inappropriately aggressive or intense for a woman; when she challenges conventional feminine sexual behavior, she is also associated with other unconventional and censured sexual proclivities.

In contrast to Marcella and Cornelia Laura plays the games of courtship and love like a man and is willing to engage in sexual intercourse before marriage. In act 3, scene 1 she mistakes Julio for Galliard in the dark and invites him into her house. While the door is open, Octavio, who mistakes Julio for Fillamour, follows along to avenge Marcella's honor. Laura, we learn in a subsequent scene, asks Julio to marry her, and he agrees, though he later confesses he only did so in order to have sex with her (5.1.232–54). Laura and Julio are on the verge of consummating their union when Octavio interrupts and draws his sword on Julio. Later, in act 5, scene 1, Laura, having learned of her mistake with Julio, repeats the attempt with the right man and is stopped only when Cornelia throws a wrench in the works. Though Laura's attempts at seduction are thwarted by last-minute plot developments instigated by other characters, her eagerness and willingness to have sex before marriage stand in sharp contrast to Marcella and Cornelia's determination to remain chaste. But Laura's audaciousness exacts a price. Marcella and Cornelia are, in the end, rewarded by marriage to Fillamour and Galliard respectively, while Laura is paired off with Julio and must accept the arranged marriage she had tried to avoid.

While Behn's greater attention to subplots involving Marcella and Cornelia enables her to create a romantic comedy in which tensions between liminal feminine power and social structure are both demonstrated and resolved, Laura's reconciliation to the concluding social order, while conforming to the generic conventions of marriage-plot comedy, is inconsistent with the will and activity she demonstrates in the play's liminal phase. In a play in which getting the right man is the goal of all the female characters, and in which arranged marriages are represented as something to avoid, Laura's union to Julio suggests a kind of censure for her sexual adventuring. Behn, however, handles this "punishment" ambiguously in the play's final scene. After Laura loses her man, she cheerfully accepts an arranged marriage, only to have her subplot abruptly dismissed as the focus of the scene shifts toward the unions between the more conventional heroines and their cavaliers. That Behn does not follow through with Laura's story suggests that there is something irresolvable about it. Equally significant, despite her best efforts Laura does not actually commit the serious sexual transgression of surrendering her virginity before marriage. In the specific social context of *The Feigned Courtesans,* in which women can only be chaste virgins or sexually active prostitutes, such an irrevocable action would be incompatible with the conventional reestablishment of an inclusive social order, one of romantic comedy's narrative goals. Through her representation of Laura, Behn asserts a self-serving feminine sexual subjectivity more powerful and more potentially disruptive than that of either of her more conventional heroines, while simultaneously highlighting the impossibility of its existence within the play's concluding patriarchal order.

At the play's conclusion all of its plot twists are untangled; the three feigned courtesans resume their proper identities in a social order successfully reestablished through the comedy's obligatory unions. The play's final scene is devoted to straightening out the confusion engendered by the heroines' liminal disguises and restoring them to circulation as goods traded by and among men rather than self-determining commodities. As Diamond puts it, "the financial stink of prostitution is hastily cleared away."[16] Octavio gives his sister Laura to Julio after Galliard testifies that she has remained "innocent" (5.4.84). Cornelia and Marcella are united with the appropriate partners but not before their guardian, Count Morosini, makes sure that they have maintained their virginity: "[P]ray give me leave to ask you a civil question: are you sure you have been honest?" (5.4.162–63). Petro admits that he has supplied the women with cash he obtained through conning the play's fools, Sir Signal Buffoon and the Reverend Tickletext, and the now-reformed Galliard declares that because the theft was committed "for the supply of two fair ladies, all shall be restored again" (5.4.197–98). Behn thus goes to some lengths to distinguish her conclusion's socially acceptable trade in women sanctioned by paternal approval from her liminal metaphor of prostitution, socially unacceptable and associated with feminine autonomy. In doing so, she restores each of her female characters to a patriarchal order in which her virtue and social standing are uncontested, but her sexual identity reverts to masculine control.

At the end of *The Feigned Courtesans* Behn's dual emphases on the construction of shared personal relationships and the reestablishment of social order result in a work in which both the heroines' and their patriarchal society's demands are ostensibly satisfied in a manner consistent with the conventions of romantic comedy. The play's women willingly give up the liminal power they exercised as courtesans, and as their virginities are confirmed and marriages approved, they are reconciled to their social order. Behn's heroines are reconciled, however, to a social order that is essentially reconstructed rather than morally altered, creating a sense of disconnection between their liminal and concluding representations. Social order, in Behn's play, depends on feminine sexualities that ultimately comply with patriarchal norms—conventional morality—while the disorder of its liminal phase is marked by oppositional femininities expressed through the socially deviant figure of the prostitute.

Throughout *The Feigned Courtesans,* as the business of prostitution is repeatedly compared to the business of marriage, Behn suggests that the only real difference between the two forms of trade in women's bodies is a matter of patriarchal regulation and paternal approval. Through this aspect of her comparison Behn manages to undermine the social order's glorification of feminine chastity and sexual passivity by representing her heroines as actively desiring women who pursue shared-love relationships in a highly sexualized context. Behn's liminal representations of her heroines argue for the recognition of an inherent and autonomous feminine sexuality within the body of the respectable virgin. The discrepancy between Marcella's vocal valorization of feminine virtue and her body's sexual allure, as well as the more forthright sexual self-representations of Cornelia and Laura, works to establish the virgin as an autonomously sexual being.

While asserting feminine sexual self-determination and desire through the liminal adventures of her heroines, Behn also exposes the significant social limitations that shape feminine sexual subjectivity by grounding her comparisons between prostitution and the marriage market in a world in which women are unquestionably economically dependent on men. Throughout the play the social and economic authority of men remains the stable backdrop against which Behn constructs her liminally active heroines. Opposition to social convention and sexual regulation grants the play's heroines a degree of autonomy, but this autonomy is predicated on the courtesan's sexual desirability and is thus enveloped within and subject to the larger social context of masculine control. While the sexual identities that Marcella and Cornelia appropriate enable them to unite with the men whom they have chosen, Laura, the most sexually autonomous and self-interested virgin, must be saved from herself in order to be successfully incorporated within the play's concluding social order. Feminine sexuality, while represented as a source of power and potential pleasure, ultimately derives both its social force and value through its gratification of masculine desire, signified by the pleasure the courtesan offers her customers, the pleasure the bride offers her husband, and the pleasure the actress offers her spectators.

The rigid oppositions between masculine social and economic dominance and feminine social dependency that structure both the liminal and concluding phases of *The Feigned Courtesans* give rise to the series of polarized oppositions (virgin/prostitute, active/passive, subject/object, compliant/deviant) that haunt Behn's constructions of femininity throughout the play. As the virgins become the courtesans, Behn manages to collapse the distinctions between the terms of these oppositions through her affirmative constructions of feminine sexual identities. The larger opposition, however, between masculine social power and feminine social powerlessness remains operative throughout the play. Although Behn plays with this opposition through liminal representational strategies of inversion as the feigned courtesans drive the play's action, the reestablishment of social order rights the balance of power and provides little opportunity for redefining feminine autonomy apart from feminine manipulation of masculine desire or shifting the values of its concluding patriarchal order. At the same time, the comedy's liminal phase reveals potentials that point beyond the conventional values its conclusion reasserts. What changes is not the conclusion's social order but its status as self-evident. At the curtain's close the play's conclusion is rendered the result of a narrative process, an effect, and the possibilities foreclosed by its reestablished order linger in the pleasures produced by its liminal confusions.

Notes

1. J. Douglas Canfield, *Tricksters and Estates: On the Ideology of Restoration Comedy* (Louisville: University Press of Kentucky, 1997), 40.

2. Northrop Frye, "Archetypal Criticism: The Theory of Myths," in *Anatomy of Criticism: Four Essays* (Princeton, NJ: Princeton University Press, 1957), 163.

3. Kathleen Rowe, *The Unruly Woman: Gender and the Genres of Laughter* (Austin: University of Texas Press, 1995), 108.

4. Derived from *limen*, Latin for "threshold," Turner's *liminality* and *liminal* are the most useful terms to describe the disorder of romantic comedy's middle phase and the representations found within it since the words themselves intimate their transitory nature. Turner suggests that the participant in the liminal phase of a ritual "passes through a cultural realm that has few or none of the attributes of the past or coming state" and argues "these persons elude or slip through the network of classifications that normally locate states and positions in cultural space. Liminal entities are neither here nor there; they are betwixt and between the positions assigned by law, custom, convention, and ceremonial" (Victor Turner, *The Ritual Process: Structure and Anti-Structure* [Chicago: Aldine De Gruyter, 1995], 94, 95).

5. Jane Spencer, "'Deceit, Dissembling, All That's Woman': Comic Plot and Female Action in *The Feigned Courtesans*," in *Rereading Aphra Behn: History, Theory, and Criticism*, ed. Heidi Hutner (Charlottesville: University Press of Virginia, 1993), 100.

6. Elin Diamond, "*Gestus*, Signature, Body in the Theater of Aphra Behn," in *Unmaking Mimesis: Essays on Feminism and Theater* (New York: Routledge, 1997), 70.

7. Aphra Behn, *The Feigned Courtesans; or, A Night's Intrigue*, in *"The Rover" and Other Plays*, ed. Jane Spencer (New York: Oxford University Press), 2.1.68.

8. Diamond, "*Gestus*, Signature, Body," 75.

9. Laura J. Rosenthal, "Reading Masks: The Actress and Spectatrix in Restoration Shakespeare," in *Broken Boundaries: Women and Feminism in Restoration Drama*, ed. Katherine M. Quinsey (Lexington: University Press of Kentucky, 1996), 207.

10. Spencer, "'Deceit, Dissembling,'" 99.

11. Katherine Maus, "'Playhouse Flesh and Blood': Sexual Ideology and the Restoration Actress," *ELH* 46 (1979): 601, 599.

12. See Susan Owen, *Restoration Theatre and Crisis* (Oxford: Clarendon, 1996), 1–3.

13. Spencer, "'Deceit, Dissembling,'" 99.

14. Rose A. Zimbardo, *A Mirror to Nature: Transformations in Drama and Aesthetics, 1660–1732* (Lexington: University Press of Kentucky, 1986), 112.

15. Harold Weber, *The Restoration Rake-Hero: Transformations in Sexual Understanding in Seventeenth-Century England* (Madison: University of Wisconsin Press, 1986), 6.

16. Diamond, "*Gestus*, Signature, Body," 62.

Solving the *Laramie* Problem, or, Projecting onto *Laramie*

Roger Freeman

THE LARAMIE PROJECT is a dramatic/theatrical work based on the 1998 murder of Matthew Shepard, a gay student at the University of Wyoming in Laramie, who was beaten and left to die by two young Laramie residents, Aaron McKinney and Russell Henderson. The brutality of the attack, which was apparently motivated, at least in part, by virulent homophobia, led to national media coverage and sparked demonstrations and calls for the enactment of hate crime legislation around the country.[1] Composed by Moisés Kaufman and members of the Tectonic Theatre Project (TTP), *The Laramie Project* consists of a range of materials relating to the event, including interviews with Laramie residents conducted by TTP members, statements from TTP members, court transcripts, public announcements from the hospital where Shepard was treated, and other texts.

Focusing on a specific historical event, and composed in part of official public documents relating to that event, *The Laramie Project* follows in the tradition of documentary theatre. Yet the dominance of statements from individuals interviewed by TTP members has led to the work's being classed with other forms, such as "theatre of testimony," as developed by Emily Mann and others. Ryan Claycomb describes *The Laramie Project*, as well as Mann's work and Anna Deavere Smith's solo performances, as "staged oral history."[2] As Claycomb describes it, one of the distinguishing features of staged oral history is "the fragmentation of narrative and perspective,"[3] a rejection of an overarching singular, third-person perspective on the events being treated in favor of multiple, first-person perspectives on those events. "Staged oral history radically fragments the unitary subject and creates montages of voice that indicate a polyphonic subjectivity."[4] Jay Baglia and Elissa Foster similarly write, "Although the telling of *The Laramie Project* is chronological . . . it violates expectations of conventional narrative through its use of multiple narrators."[5]

The Laramie Project, in fact, deviates from traditional narrative—and dramatic—structure in several important ways. As Claycomb and Baglia and Foster note, the use of multiple narrators distinguishes *The Laramie Project* from works presented from the third-person objective perspective that Hayden White and others have described as a signal characteristic of narrative representation. White, citing Gérard Genette, observes that within narrative, "the events seem to tell themselves" rather than being presented from a particular subjective position, let alone several such positions.[6] This refusal of a singular, authoritative position is reinforced by the particular content and arrangement of the various interviews, which, though all related to or motivated by the attack and its aftermath, range freely over a variety of topics. As a consequence the work deviates from traditional narrative structure in two other crucial, related ways: the absence of a specific, definitive central subject (in narrative terms) and the absence of definitive closure. These deviations from narrative structure give rise to what has been seen by some as a problem: the failure to deliver an unambiguous meaning or moral lesson. This essay examines how this "problem" has been perceived and how particular moral perspectives have been projected onto the text to redress it.

That *The Laramie Project* lacks a definitive central subject is illustrated by attempts to describe just what the work is about. Amy Tigner, in her article "*The Laramie Project*: Western Pastoral," identifies in the text features common to the pastoral poem and to the American western, which she presents as a modern version of the pastoral.[7] In the pastoral, Tigner writes, "those from the epitome of civilization leave society and enter into a wilderness, a rural landscape, or a pasture, and then disguise themselves as local country folk" and tell stories about "societal problems" (140). In the case of the pastoral elegy the story is often about a lost shepherd. In the western "the cultured outsider . . . comes to the West to flee the burden of industrialization and slowly begins to take on the costume and the customs of the 'untamed' Westerner" (140). Clearly, both of these descriptions apply to *The Laramie Project*, which deals not only with the murder of Matthew Shepard but also with the particular experiences of the members of TTP as they conducted their work. Yet as Tigner explains, in the pastoral elegy the central figure is the shepherd of whom the cultured outsider speaks, whereas in the western it is the cultured outsider himself. This shift in the central subject can be found elsewhere in Tigner's essay: at one point Matthew Shepard is presented as the "heroic yet tragic figure" (140) of *The Laramie Project;* at another point Aaron Kreifels, who found Shepard, "becomes a romantic hero" (144).

Tigner states, "As a pastoral elegy, *The Laramie Project* tells of the community attempting to come together after the tragic death of Matt Shepard" (141). This statement is only partially correct. Certain passages do show a community attempting to come together, but Tigner's description is not representative of the entire piece. The difficulty in pinning down just what *The Laramie Project* is about is also suggested by Baglia and Foster, who write that *The Laramie Project* "is not about Shepard so much as it is about how a community identifies itself in the wake of the national media coverage of a hate crime."[8] This statement comes close to Tigner's assertion that *The Laramie Project* "tells of the community attempting to come together," but here the catalyst is the media coverage rather than the murder itself. That *The Laramie Project* possesses no single central subject is also suggested by the conjunction Baglia and Foster use: "so much as."

Tigner also states earlier in her essay that *The Laramie Project* "chronicles the story of Matthew Shepard's death" (139). This is also only partially correct, but it is closer to the mark in that *The Laramie Project* is more a chronicle than a narrative. White notes that a chronicle typically deals with a central subject—"the life of an individual, town, or region"—but that the chronicle has traditionally been regarded as "something less than a fully realized [narrative] history" because it takes (mere) "chronology as the organizing principle of the discourse" and as a result "does not so much conclude as simply terminate; typically it lacks closure, that summing up of the 'meaning' of the chain of events with which it deals that we normally expect from the well-made story."[9] In a sense, then, *The Laramie Project* has a central subject, but it is not the kind of central subject that narrative typically traffics in.

That *The Laramie Project* lacks narrative closure is suggested by Baglia and Foster's essay. In response to a production they attended, they write, "As drama, *The Laramie Project* felt like a complete account, and we walked away with a sense of closure as audience members; it provided the resolution we expect from a well-told story."[10] Nevertheless, they do not specify what the complete account *was of* or *what* was brought to closure. More interesting is what they did not find: meaning. In *The Laramie Project* Baglia and Foster found a reflection of a general tendency in American society "to turn to the news for facts, facts, and more facts" in the face of crises. They continue: "Facts, however, do not supply us with meaning. . . . What we wanted was a truth that transformed the meaning of Shepard's murder from one town's tragedy into an awakening of the nation's conscience" (136). To illustrate what they found lacking in *The Laramie Project*, they refer approvingly to another American play dealing with a specific historical event, writing, "What *The Crucible* offers us that *The Laramie Project* does not is a metaphor that penetrates the heart of a particular event in American history without limiting its interpretation to that single event" (140).

As the reference to *The Crucible* suggests, it is narrative, with its tight objective focus on a particular subject and its clear resolution, that generates meaning. White writes, "Common opinion has it that the plot of a narrative imposes a meaning on the events that make up its story level by revealing at the end a structure that was immanent in the events all along."[11] Moreover, such meaning is bound up with morality. That the meaning of a story is imbued with morality is succinctly suggested by William Gass's pithy comment, "I've yet to meet a moral that really was."[12] Narrative is the "moral order," the structure that conveys a meaning. It is also the "moralizing order." White writes:

> If every fully realized story, however we define that familiar but conceptually elusive entity, is a kind of allegory, points to a moral, or endows events, whether real or imaginary, with a significance that they do not possess as mere sequence, then it seems possible to conclude that every historical narrative has as its latent or manifest purpose the desire to moralize the events of which it treats.... And this suggests that narrativity, certainly in factual storytelling and probably in fictional storytelling as well, is intimately related to, if not a function of, the impulse to moralize reality, that is, to identify it with the social system that is the source of any morality that we can imagine.[13]

Baglia and Foster's disappointment with *The Laramie Project* for failing to provide a meaning or moral, despite the sense of closure that it provided, seems clearly to arise from a sense of the text's impartiality, a result of the fragmentation of narrative and perspective, that Claycomb identifies. Tigner and Claycomb both rightly observe that *The Laramie Project* is a product not only of interviewing but of editing, and editing can, of course, serve a moralizing function. Baglia and Foster, writing largely from an ethnographic perspective, also comment on the editing process and its effects. They report feeling some "slight uneasiness regarding how certain citizens of Laramie had been represented" in a production they attended and note that by "selecting and arranging the words of the characters, the TTP grants life to some of the citizens of Laramie and silences others."[14]

Despite these concerns, however, Baglia and Foster clearly perceived in *The Laramie Project* at least an attempt to maintain a neutral position on the arguments presented. In fact, they criticize the piece for its apparent "ethos of neutrality" (128), a phrase they borrow from Claycomb. And their disappointment with the work for failing to provide meaning is followed by a call for "documentary theatre to loosen its claim of truth, its grasp on objectivity, and its implied political neutrality."[15] So, all caveats regarding the shaping of its source material notwithstanding, there is in some quarters a sense that the multiple and sometimes conflicting testimonies that make up *The Laramie Project* are presented impartially and that this creates a problem, namely that the piece is not sufficiently moralizing. I will argue in the remaining pages that the text has also apparently been seen by others as insufficiently moralizing in the more familiar sense of promoting a particular moral position. This perception of the neutrality of the text, or at least portions of it, has led to production choices that privilege a particular moral perspective on the statements contained in the text. The primary illustrations for this argument come from the 2002 HBO special, directed by Moisés Kaufman. Brief reference will also be made to a 2004 stage production in Syracuse, New York. Throughout, these illustrations will be compared to the text published by Vintage Press in 2001.

The HBO special ("the special") is substantially different from the Vintage text ("the text") in terms of the selection and arrangement of material. This should not be taken as a suggestion that the text is a more "authentic" representation of events than is the special. In fact, while at points the text seems to offer a more accurate depiction of events than does the special, at other points the opposite may be true. In any event the special employs particular devices to establish or reinforce a particular moral position on specific passages that, in the text, are presented rather impartially. This can be seen in the treatment of three specific interviews, which in both the special and the text appear very closely together. The first is with Sherry Johnson, the wife of a Laramie police officer. The second is with a Catholic priest, Father Roger Schmit. The third is with a Baptist minister, who at his own request remains unnamed.

In the text the scene with Sherry Johnson is a monologue, reproduced below in its entirety:

> I really haven't been all that involved, per se. My husband's a highway patrolman, so that's really the only way that I've known about it.
> Now when I first found out I just thought it was horrible. I just, I can't . . . Nobody deserves that! I don't care who ya are.
> But, the other thing that was not brought out—at the same time this

happened that patrolman was killed. And there was nothing. Nothing. They didn't say anything about the old man that killed him. He was driving down the road and he shouldn't have been driving and he killed him. It was just a little piece in the paper. And we lost one of our guys.

You know, my husband worked with him. This man was brand-new on the force. But, I mean, here's one of ours, and it was just a little piece in the paper.

And a lot of it is my feeling that the media is portraying Matthew Shepard as a saint. And making him as a martyr. And I don't think he was. I don't think he was that pure.

Now, I didn't know him, but . . . there's just so many things about him that I found out that I just, it's scary. You know about his character and spreading AIDS and a few other things, you know, being the kind of person that he was. He was, he was just a barfly, you know. And I think he pushed himself around. I think he flaunted it.

Everybody's got problems. But why they exemplified him I don't know. What's the difference if you're gay? A hate crime is a hate crime. If you murder somebody you hate 'em. It has nothing to do with if you're gay or a prostitute or whatever.

I don't understand. I don't understand.[16]

As recorded in the text, then, the scene is a good example of Baglia and Foster's observation of how *The Laramie Project* follows the practices of documentary reporting: "just as the conventions of documentary keep the questioner off-screen, we do not get to hear the questions asked of Laramie residents."[17]

In the special Johnson's statements come in a different order and are broken up by questions and statements from TTP interviewer Leigh Fondakowski (played by Kelli Simpkins). The sequence remains the same, aside from a couple of inconsequential details, through "Nobody deserves that. I don't care who ya are." This is followed by a shot of Simpkins tilting her head slightly forward while maintaining a fixed, neutral expression. Johnson's statement about the media portrayal of Shepard follows. Her sentence "And I don't think he was [a martyr]" is followed by a question from Fondakowski: "Did you know him?" This leads to Johnson's admission that she did not know Shepard and her comments about his "character." (This segment includes one interjection from Fondakowski, who responds to Johnson's allusion to "the kind of person [Shepard] was" with, "Meaning?") Johnson's comments regarding the amount of attention given to the police officer's death come next and are followed by a statement from Fondakowski, "But this was such a deliberate crime." After a pause, in which Johnson is portrayed as confused by the statement, Laura Linney as Johnson continues, "Everybody's got problems. Why they're exemplifying Matthew Shepard I don't know. A hate crime's a hate crime. You murder somebody you hate 'em. It has nothing to do if you're a [*sic*] gay or a prostitute or I—I don't know."[18] This statement is followed by a shot of Fondakowski staring tight-lipped back at Johnson, a faint twitch in Simpkins's cheek conveying disapproval. Linney then delivers the last two lines, which seem to acquire a more global resonance as a result of the preceding shot of the interviewer: "I don't understand. I don't understand."

In the text the next scene, an interview with Father Roger Schmit, includes some comments from the interviewers, Fondakowski and Greg Pierotti, and these are retained in the special. In the special, as in the text, the scene is preceded by Pierotti's announcing that they are about to interview Father Schmit and saying, "Here we go. Two queers and a Catholic priest." At the top of the interview the special depicts Pierotti and Fondakowski as being a bit confused by Father Schmit's statement, "Matthew Shepard has served us well," but they soon regain their composure and appear gratified by Father Schmit's description of how he helped arrange a vigil without seeking the bishop's approval. They are also shown as being reassured and touched by his statement, "They did do violence to Matthew—but you know every time that you are called a fag, or you are called a you know, a lez or whatever . . . Do you realize that is violence? That is the seed of violence."

In the text this interview ends with Father Schmit saying, "Just deal with what is true. You know what is true. You need to do your best to say it correct."[19] The special retains these lines in this order but capitalizes on the conventions of film to shift the location to a motel room, where TTP members are shown listening to the recording of the interview. The statement "You know what is true" is made directly by Father Schmit in his office; the last statement, "You need to do your best to say it correct," comes from a tape recorder in the motel room while soft music plays.

The following sections of the special are particularly illuminating. In the text the interview with Father Schmit is followed by a monologue from Andrew Gomez, who describes spending time with Aaron McKinney in jail and explains how he had heard that McKinney and Henderson were already being auctioned off at the prison where they were to be sent. In the special this scene is cut entirely, and the scene in the motel room is followed by a segment that is not in the text. This segment features TTP member Amanda Gronich (played by Clea Duvall) explaining, "These people trust us. You know, they want—they want everyone to know that they are not this crime. And it's more than clearing Laramie's name; it's clearing their own, and I don't know that we can do that." This segment is followed by an interview with the Baptist Minister, who was introduced earlier in the text and in the special delivering a sermon in which he identifies himself as a Biblicist and asserts, "The word is either sufficient or it is not."[20] This portion of the special is particularly interesting because it depicts an interview that actually took place over the telephone as having been a face-to-face encounter on a sidewalk outside of a Laramie cafe. Michael Emerson plays the Baptist Minister as distinctly callous, placing special emphasis on the words *reflect* and *lifestyle* in the line, "I hope . . . that before [Shepard] slipped into a coma he had a chance to reflect on his lifestyle." He ends this line with a grimace. A long pause follows, during which Gronich is portrayed as stunned but finally able to force out the words, "Thank you, Reverend. I appreciate your speaking to me." The Baptist Minister remains impassive and merely says, "All right. We better go," before leading his wife down the sidewalk, leaving Gronich standing slump-shouldered in swirling snow. (The script calls for rain to start falling on the stage at the end of this segment.)[21] After the minister excuses himself and departs, the special features a shot of some of Gronich's fellow company members looking out through the front window of the cafe. The special does not show Gronich entering the cafe, but the very next segment shows her emerging through the door of the cafe back onto the sidewalk with Kaufman (Nestor Carbonell) close behind. Out on the sidewalk she says, "I let him say that to me. I let him say that to me, and I didn't say anything back." Kaufman attempts to console her, but, obviously distraught and approaching tears, she pushes him back and heads down the street alone.

In light of the scene with Father Schmit this scene is, put mildly, amusing. In the special the interview with Father Schmit is cast in a highly positive light, and the emphasis laid on his insistence that the members of TTP know what is true, should deal with what is true, and need to do their best to say it correct suggests that the true and the correct are exactly what *The Laramie Project* is after. Within minutes an interview that was conducted by telephone is presented as a face-to-face encounter and is tagged with a miniscene that not only is not in the text but may never have happened. In a discussion at Berkeley Repertory Theatre in 2001 Amanda Gronich, referring to this interview, said, "I felt slimy. I got off the phone and never said anything."[22] Perhaps Gronich spoke the words contained in the HBO special to someone after the fact, but her comments at Berkeley Rep suggest that it wasn't right after the fact.

A production at the Syracuse Civic Theatre seems to have adopted a similar approach to this scene. Reviewer James MacKillop reports that the performance featured "the icy words of the Baptist Minister who prays that Shepard had a chance to reflect on his sinful lifestyle during the 18 hours he spent lashed to the fencepost. At this a female interviewer is portrayed in tearful revulsion."[23] Actually, in the text the Baptist Minister is never shown praying. This, however, is a minor point. Of greater interest is the observation that the minister's "icy words" left the interviewer in "tearful revulsion." If MacKillop perceived the Baptist Minister's words as icy, this probably had something to do with how they were delivered. More to the point, though, is the reference to the interviewer in tearful revulsion. As in the special, the Syracuse production appears to have presented Gronich as the victim of a violent, hateful verbal assault.

My concerns about editing have already been noted. Here both HBO and the Syracuse Civic Theatre entered the realm of editorializing. Claycomb writes that "the issue of hate crime legislation, which seems to have the support of the acting company members, is given an equally compelling refutation by a police officer's wife, whose voice is . . . left unmediated by the acting company. That is, even though the actor playing Sherry Johnson delivers the monologue, this voice is not undermined by narration or by a staged interviewer who might challenge her claims."[24] Yet Claycomb appends a note: "I offer this with its own caveat, since the 2002 HBO production of the play portrays this character as narrow-minded and ignorant, a sense I do not get from the text of the play" (121). Johnson does come off as narrow-minded and ignorant in the HBO special, but the special may at least be recreating the actual conditions and features of the interview. It interpolates comments from the interviewer that do not appear in the text, but those interpolations may well have been part of the interview in the first place. Moreover, the statement that earns Johnson a fixed stare in the HBO special, "It doesn't matter if you're gay or a prostitute or whatever," is in fact in the text. The telephone interview with the Baptist Minister not only is presented as a face-to-face encounter that makes the actor's already callous portrayal seem even more mean-spirited, but it is also followed by a textual interpolation that reinforces the presumed savagery of his words. On this point, though, Claycomb is silent.

It's not that Claycomb doesn't mention the Baptist Minister at all. In fact, he sees the minister "using his time with the interviewer to condemn homosexuality as he would in the pulpit" (116). This assertion demands some scrutiny. In an earlier telephone interview, responding to Gronich's statement, "I was extremely interested in talking with the reverend about some of his thoughts about recent events," the minister's wife says, "Well, I don't think he'll want to talk to you. He has very biblical views about homosexuality—he doesn't condone that kind of violence. But he doesn't condone that kind of lifestyle, you know what I mean."[25] In the text the minister refers to homosexuality only once, during his interview with Gronich: "Now, as for the victim, I know that that lifestyle is legal, but I will tell you one thing: I hope that Matthew Shepard as he was tied to that fence, that he had time to reflect on a moment when someone had spoken the word of the Lord to him— and that before he slipped into a coma he had a chance to reflect on his lifestyle."[26] Without question, these words recall the Baptist Minister's wife's statement that he "doesn't condone that kind of lifestyle," and indicate that the minister disapproves of homosexuality. That evident disapproval notwithstanding, however, the statement does not primarily seem to be a condemnation. It appears just as likely, if not more so, that the Baptist Minister is expressing a sincere hope for the salvation of Shepard's soul. The text itself suggests this. Just before the passage quoted above, the Baptist Minister says to Gronich:

> Now, those two people, the accused, have forfeited their lives. We've been after the two I mentioned for ages, trying to get them to live right, to do right. Now, one boy is on suicide watch and I am working with him—until they put him in the chair and turn on the juice I will work for his salvation. Now I think they deserve the death penalty—I will try to deal with them spiritually.[27]

Though believing that the assailants deserve to die for their actions, the Baptist Minister says that he is committed to working toward their salvation. In the special all that remains of this passage is the final sentence. The special and seemingly the Syracuse production depicted the Baptist Minister's words as hateful and contemptible. It may well be that the words were meant hatefully, but the text does not allow such a definitive conclusion. The text clearly indicates that the Baptist Minister regards homosexuality as a sin, but it provides no evidence that he does not endorse the belief, held by many Christians, that one must "love the sinner but hate the sin."[28] In any event, regardless of whether one shares or endorses the Baptist Minister's beliefs, it seems only fair to consider that, rather than condemning homosexuality, his words represent his hope that Shepard had repented of his sins and had received the gift of eternal life. In the light of the minister's statement that he will be working for the salvation of men who in his view deserve to die, this seems as legitimate an interpretation of the words as any other. The devices and tactics employed by the special and the Syracuse production to depict a victimized Gronich all but guarantee that this more sympathetic interpretation will remain unavailable to their audiences.

The HBO special and, it seems, the Syracuse production villainized the Baptist Minister, apparently because of a sense that his words were hateful and condemnatory. There is another Baptist minister in *The Laramie Project*, and it seems odd that those scholars who have chosen to defend one or the other of these men have picked Fred Phelps. Claycomb states, "the play villainizes the Reverend Fred Phelps and company."[29] Baglia and Foster write that they "were introduced to a cartoon version of the homophobic and bigoted Reverend Fred Phelps, and, as audience members, we wanted the TTP to talk to Phelps, not just lampoon him."[30] While it may have been illuminating to see an actual encounter between Phelps and the TTP, it is not in fact clear that the text—or the HBO special—villainizes or lampoons Phelps at all. Phelps is merely presented as he is—a man who crows about God's hate. Nothing in the text is any more exaggerated than the contents of the Westboro Baptist Church's Web site, www.godhatesfags.com, where one can find a page containing a "Perpetual Gospel Memorial to Matthew Shepard." This page, which is updated every day, features a picture of Shepard surrounded by flames; it also includes text informing the viewer (as of May 1, 2006), "Matthew Shepard has been in hell for 2,759 days. Eternity—2,759 days = Eternity"; accompanying audio allows the viewer to listen to "Matthew's message from hell," a tortured voice screaming, "For God's sake, listen to Phelps." (A similar memorial to Diane Whipple can be found at the same site.) Nor is anything in the text more exaggerated than the contents of WBC's other site, www.godhatesamerica.com, where one can find photos of WBC members picketing the funerals of dead soldiers with signs reading, "Thank God for dead soldiers" and "Thank God for IEDs." Among other claims, the site explains that the tsunami that devastated Southeast Asia happened because God hates Sweden.

Baglia and Foster perceive in the HBO special a "self-referential quality that made the story more like a 'making of' special rather than a film of the play."[31] They give the special some credit for "reveal[ing] more of the created, constructed aspects of *The Laramie Project*," but they also state that they "felt even further removed from the genealogy of the story." They also credit the special for giving "more of a detailed picture of the internal struggles of the TTP members as they came to terms with their own fears and their complicity, while trying to remain objective in the face of glaring bigotry and homophobia." "But," they continue, "the narrative had lost its anchor—was this film about Laramie, Matthew Shepard, TTP, hate crime legislation, or perhaps how liberal and socially conscious HBO is?" (137). Baglia and Foster are exactly right when they write that it is not clear what the HBO special is *about*, but the statement that "the narrative had lost its anchor" begs the question: just what is "*the* story" or "*the* narrative" of *The Laramie Project* in the first place?

Baglia and Foster's reservations about the HBO special are justified; the special seems to be at least as much about its own making as it is about anything else. Yet, at least in the segments featuring Sherry Johnson, Father Schmit, Amanda Gronich, and the Baptist Minister, it is not clear that the narrative loses its anchor. Rather the treatment of these sections of the text suggests an effort to endow the work with some of the features of narrative, casting it as a kind of morality tale that depicts a confrontation between the forces of good and evil, or at least of enlightenment and ignorance. White notes that

> we cannot but be struck by the frequency with which narrativity, whether of the fictional or factual sort, presupposes the existence of a legal system against which or on behalf of which the typical agents of a narrative account militate. And this raises the suspicion that narrative in general, from the folktale to the novel, from the annals to the fully realized "history," has to do with the topics of law, legality, legitimacy, or, more generally, authority.[32]

For "legal system" one could substitute "moral order" and maintain the same basic argument. What the HBO special and the Syracuse production suggest is a sense that the text, lacking a single and unified moral narrative, is insufficiently moralizing on its own and requires a boost to make its presumed, or hoped-for, morality evident.

Tigner, Claycomb, and Baglia and Foster all refer to community in their essays on *The Laramie Project*. The subject of community is especially important to Claycomb, who observes that the term can be applied in at least four ways: "1) as the larger represented community of all voices in the play; 2) as smaller represented communities that can be grouped together by perspective or by ideology; 3) as the community of actors who represent these first two communities; and 4) as the community of audience members and actors who together experience an individual theatrical event."[33] Claycomb argues that "part of the goal of [oral history] plays seems . . . to establish in the city at large a dialogue that engenders more meaningful connections across the smaller, more insular communities that it harbors, a goal that many of these plays, in fact, accomplish" (100). He also argues that "the goal of these oral histories [seems to be] to create in the audience a sense of community that encourages dialogue, that allows for the peaceful confrontation of individual identities and that incorporates them all into the utopian space of the theatre" (104).

Claycomb's observation that within any large community one may find smaller communities bound less by geographical proximity than by perspective or ideology is important because it problematizes any statements that *The Laramie Project* tells about or depicts a community attempting to come together or identify itself in the wake of a crime. *Which* community is attempting to come together?[34] Sherry Johnson clearly feels that her community ("And we lost one of our guys") has been marginalized in the wake of the reaction to Shepard's murder. The Baptist Minister warns his congregation that they will be mocked for their faith.[35] Other members of the "larger represented community" of Laramie likewise assert that they and their beliefs are being marginalized or ignored. Thus, any claim that *The Laramie Project* is about, or tells of, a community identifying itself or attempting to come together can gain purchase only by excluding particular figures from the community or by positioning them as noxious elements against which the (legitimate) community militates.

As I have acknowledged, *The Laramie Project* is the result of much editing and shaping, and some voices and perspectives—including moral perspectives—are given more space than others, but the particular strength of the text is that it does not moralize.[36] Even those individuals who appear small in the text at least seem to have had their words accurately recorded. For this reason the work has the potential to create in the theatre what Claycomb describes: a peaceful confrontation of individual identities from the insular communities that the city harbors. But Claycomb's utopian vision of the theatre should be placed against Baglia and Foster's suspicion that "*The Laramie Project* confirms for liberal audiences what they already believe—that violence and hatred are wrong."[37] This statement hints at the possibility that the peaceful confrontation that Claycomb envisions will largely be between like-minded people who didn't have much to argue about in the first place.

Baglia and Foster's reference to *liberal* audiences in particular is interesting. It does not seem self-evident that the belief that violence and hatred are wrong is the exclusive property of liberal audiences. More to the point, it seems difficult, if not impossible, within the larger American social context, to invoke the term *liberal* without summoning up, whether intentionally or not, its familiar foil, *conservative*. One might ask how the terms of this polarity slipped into the discussion of *The Laramie Project*, along with the sense that it is liberal audiences in particular who will find their prejudices being reaffirmed. The HBO special and the Syracuse production suggest an answer, which is that some actors and directors, confronting a text that does not conform to the moral order of narrative, have found other means to privilege one moral order above another by creating a villainous "they" that the virtuous "we" must stand against.[38] This may be reassuring, in the way that melodrama reassures, but there's no reason to expect to see those who identify with the putative villains in the theatre, at least after the second intermission. Reducing *The Laramie Project* to a morality tale comes at a price, and it is more than an aesthetic price. The utopia that Claycomb envisions will likely end up looking and sounding like an echo chamber.

Claycomb notes that Cornell West praises Anna Deavere Smith's neutrality in *Fires in the Mirror*. West states, "Not to choose 'sides' is itself a choice—yet to view the crisis as simply and solely a matter of choosing sides is to reduce the history and complexity of the crisis in a vulgar Manichean manner."[39] Yet as HBO clearly understands, Manichaeanism, for all its dangers, has one thing going for it—it is morally unambiguous.

Notes

1. Homophobia seems clearly to have been a motivating factor behind the beating but may not have been the only one. See JoAnn Wypijewski, "A Boy's Life: For Matthew Shepard's Killers, What Does It Take to Pass as a Man?" *Harper's Magazine,* Sep. 1999, 61–74.

2. Ryan Claycomb, "(Ch)oral History: Documentary Theatre, the Communal Subject, and Progressive Politics," *Journal of Dramatic Theory and Criticism* 17, no. 2 (spring 2003): 96.

3. Ibid., 97.

4. Ibid.

5. Jay Baglia and Elissa Foster, "Performing the 'Really' Real: Cultural Criticism, Representation, and Commodification in *The Laramie Project*," *Journal of Dramatic Theory and Criticism* 19, no. 2 (spring 2005): 131.

6. Gérard Genette, "Boundaries of Narrative," *New Literary History* 8, no. 1 (1978): 11; quoted in Hayden White, *The Content of the Form: Narrative Discourse and Historical Representation* (Baltimore: Johns Hopkins University Press, 1987), 3. As White describes it, the discernible presence of a narrator is more commonly a feature of the chronicle. There is something akin here to Aristotle's distinction between epic and dramatic poetry; the former relies on a narrator, whereas the latter consists of the "persons who are performing the imitation acting, that is, carrying on for themselves" (Aristotle, *Poetics,* trans. Gerald Else [Ann Arbor: University of Michigan Press, 1967], 18).

7. Amy Tigner, "*The Laramie Project:* Western Pastoral," *Modern Drama* 45, no. 1 (spring 2002): 138–56.

8. Baglia and Foster, "Performing the 'Really' Real," 129.

9. White, *The Content of the Form,* 16. There is another echo of Aristotle here, namely Aristotle's privileging of an imitation of an action that is complete and whole (i.e., possessing a beginning, middle, and end) over an imitation of a life: "But a plot is not unified . . . simply because it has to do with a single person. A large, indeed an indefinite number of things can happen to an individual, some of which go to constitute no unified event; and in the same way there can be many acts of a given individual from which no single action emerges" (Aristotle, *Poetics,* 31).

10. Baglia and Foster, "Performing the 'Really' Real," 131–32.

11. White, *The Content of the Form,* 20. David Carr likewise notes that one of the features of narrative is that "only from the perspective of the end do the beginning and the middle make sense" (David Carr, *Time, Narrative, and History* [Bloomington: Indiana University Press, 1986], 7).

12. William Gass, *Tests of Time* (Chicago: University of Chicago Press, 2003), 6.

13. White, *The Content of the Form,* 14.

14. Baglia and Foster, "Performing the 'Really' Real," 130, 140.

15. Ibid., 140. This reference to the implied political neutrality of documentary theatre is curious, given that one of the earliest proponents of documentary theatre, Peter Weiss, specified that "Documentary Theatre takes sides" (see Peter Weiss, "The Material and the Models: Notes Towards a Definition of Documentary Theatre," trans. Heinz Bernard, *Theatre Quarterly* 1, no. 1 [Jan.–March 1971]: 42).

16. Moisés Kaufman and the Members of the Tectonic Theater Project, *The Laramie Project* (New York: Vintage, 2001), 64–65.

17. Baglia and Foster, "Performing the 'Really' Real," 135.

18. HBO Films, *The Laramie Project* (2002). All references are based on the DVD.

19. Kaufman et al., *The Laramie Project,* 66.

20. Ibid., 23.

21. Ibid., 69.

22. Dan Fost, "Cast of 'Laramie Project' Shares a Few Journalistic Lessons," *San Francisco Chronicle,* June 27, 2001.

23. James MacKillop, "Anatomy of a Murder: *The Laramie Project* Seeks to Understand the Gruesome Death of Matthew Shepard," *Syracuse New Times,* June 9, 2004.

24. Claycomb, "(Ch)oral History," 115–16.

25. Kaufman et al., *The Laramie Project,* 27. In the HBO special the Baptist minister's wife appears only as a nonspeaking, and almost unseen, figure on the sidewalk during the encounter with Gronich.

26. Ibid., 69.

27. Ibid., 68.

28. Interestingly enough, in the special, though not in the text, Aaron Kreifels is shown stating, "I was brought up to love the sinner, hate the sin." This is tempered by his next sentence: "Love the person for who they are but condemn them for what they do—condemn the lifestyle," but it bears noting

that many Christians, including many Baptists, would object strenuously to the suggestion that one should condemn the person rather than his or her actions. In preparing this chapter, I spoke with ministers of two churches, at least one of whom would likely be regarded by most Americans as highly conservative in his beliefs. I quoted, without any preface, the Kreifels statement from the HBO special and asked for a response. Both responded immediately that one should not condemn the person at all. One stated that Jesus's command to his followers in Matthew, "Judge not that ye be not judged," could fairly be rendered as, "Condemn not that ye be not condemned."

29. Claycomb, "(Ch)oral History," 115.
30. Baglia and Foster, "Performing the 'Really' Real," 141.
31. Ibid., 136.
32. White, *The Content of the Form*, 13.
33. Claycomb, "(Ch)oral History," 100.
34. At the beginning of the Vintage text police detective Sergeant Hing describes the different communities one can find in Laramie. The HBO special left this out.
35. Kaufman et al., *The Laramie Project*, 25. This segment does not appear in the HBO special, possibly because mocking the man and showing him declaring that he would be mocked created an irony that the makers of the special considered too overt.
36. *Particular* is a key word here. I share Baglia and Foster's admiration for *The Crucible*, and I have no desire to place either *The Laramie Project* or *The Crucible* in a position of privilege. Each has its particular strengths.
37. Baglia and Foster, "Performing the 'Really' Real," 139.
38. See Claycomb, "(Ch)oral History," esp. 111.
39. Quoted in ibid., 115.

The Advantage of Controversy

Angels in America and Campus Culture Wars

James Fisher

IN AN ESSAY IN the *Nation* called "Fighting the Art Bullies," a response to controversy over the premiere production of Terrence McNally's *Corpus Christi* at the Manhattan Theatre Club, Pulitzer Prize–winning dramatist Tony Kushner nails it. He wonders, "Would a God who gave us powers of creation, curiosity and love then command us to avoid the ideas and art these powers produce?"[1] The response of any reasonable person is no, of course, even though the censorious, mostly on the political right, seem to think otherwise. As Kushner explains, they are apparently "too shallow and too fragile to encounter any interrogatory spirit," and the war against art in the name of God, decency, and civic stability that they are waging "isn't decent; it's thuggish, its unconstitutional, undemocratic and deeply unwise."[2] Hardly a week has passed in the last two decades without media reports on yet another arts controversy. Supporters of free expression in a democratic society point to the inevitable progress and human growth inherent in challenging works of art, while worrying, often appropriately so, that carefully orchestrated attacks in the name of morality could have a permanent impact on the ability to create.

Pat Buchanan's 1992 assertion that a seismic struggle is in progress for "the soul of America . . . a cultural war, as critical to the kind of nation we will one day be as was the Cold War itself" was certainly prophetic, but it is a struggle that I believe is not ending as Buchanan envisioned.[3] How did this culture war begin? Was it a product of the Reagan era? Or did it truly begin with Allan Bloom's *The Closing of the American Mind*, a 1987 best seller in which Bloom asserts that "[c]ulture means a war against chaos *and* a war against other cultures."[4] Conservatives like Buchanan and Bloom are fixated on a vision of a once homogeneous past (real or imagined) and deny that society is in a continual unstoppable process of change. Buchanan, Bloom, and their followers condemn the presentation of what they refer to as "deviant" or noncanonical texts and art; they claim, as Lawrence W. Levine explains in *The Opening of the American Mind,* Levine's counterattack on Bloom, to control a monopoly on the canon.[5]

Artists, like academics, are rightly in the business of attempting to understand and depict cultural evolution and the progress toward a more democratic, more diverse social fabric; taking strong and controversial positions is, in fact, a well-worn tradition for artists and scholars— and it is a tradition to be defended at all costs. When the overheated hyperbole of the censorious condemns artists and scholars as immoral or as leading a war of aggression against Western culture, they merely underscore that changes are, in fact, occurring and will inevitably reshape the American moral and intellectual landscape. The fear of change—which to the censorious means a loss of control and power over society—has led to organized, well-funded assaults on selected artists and academics presenting or teaching controversial works. The result has inspired genuine threats to everything from the survival of the National Endowment of the Arts to freedom of speech on college campuses. Jane Alexander, former chairperson of the NEA during its struggle for survival, suggests that controversy is the price paid for democracy.[6] If Alexander is right, and I think she is, artists are paying much of the price and will, I suspect, continue to bear the costs of vitriolic and increasingly desperate attacks.

I learned about all of this from personal experience. In 1995 I found myself caught up in a culture wars skirmish that has caused me to consider both the constructive and destructive aspects of controversy to moral debate. Choosing to stage *Millennium Approaches,* the first play of Tony Kushner's *Angels in America,* at Wabash College, a small (825 students), all-male, liberal arts college in a rural midwestern town in a decidedly red state, may suggest that on some level I was courting controversy, but I went into this experience with no idea of what I would encounter. That may seem naïve—and perhaps I was—but I merely thought I had found an important new American drama by a major voice and wished to challenge my students and myself in the process of producing it. No more, no less. But my naïveté abruptly ended while introducing Kushner for a 1995 public lecture at Wabash exactly one year before the production. I announced that our Theatre Department would stage *Millennium Approaches* in October 1996 as the opening production of our 1996–97 theatre season. Immediately following this announcement, it became all too clear that I had unwittingly fired the first shot in a culture wars battle that engulfed the college for a full year and beyond. In fact, the controversy and its outcome changed the institution, and my own life and work, for over a decade, with no end in sight.

Now when I suggest that I unwittingly found myself caught up in the culture wars, I mean that at the time, I had directed plays at Wabash for nearly twenty years without controversy. Our department had one overriding guideline: within a four-year period—a student's time at the college—as wide a variety of plays as possible would be presented. Individuals had not liked one play or another over the years, but no one had ever suggested censoring a work. In fact, Wabash prided itself on an intellectual rigor that came from challenging debate. During my years at the college we had staged a wide variety of contemporary and classic plays. Works with controversial reputations (*Lysistrata, Mrs. Warren's Profession, Loot, Marat/Sade, True West, Glengarry Glen Ross, Breaking the Code, Accidental Death of an Anarchist, Gross Indecency: The Three Trials of Oscar Wilde*) were occasionally chosen, many rife with strong language, flashes of nudity, and depictions of sexuality, including a graphically staged male-on-male rape scene in a production of John Herbert's *Fortune and Men's Eyes*. Many of our productions had also presented what some might describe as radical political or moral viewpoints, but no one had ever raised a significant complaint. Ever. In fact, my colleagues and I believed we were *expected* to present diverse views and challenging plays. So what had changed by the mid-1990s to make a production of *Millennium Approaches* tantamount to institutional treason and a violation of, as one outraged alumnus put it, "all of the values we hold dear"?

Here are the bare facts of the controversy: shortly after my introducing Kushner at his Wabash lecture and announcing the forthcoming production, the president of the College, Andrew T. Ford, invited me to lunch, ostensibly to become more acquainted with the Theatre Department's workings. Instead, Ford questioned me exclusively about the choice of the play: "How did the department choose it?" "Why do you want to do this particular play?" "Why now and not later?" "Mightn't the play's homosexual content cause confusion to students—young men at the blooming of their sexuality?" He also expressed concern about how a far right-wing student publication called the *Commentary*, aping the style of the *Dartmouth Review*, might exploit it. The *Commentary* had been bombarding alumni with distorted accounts of virtually every so-called liberal, multicultural, or gender-oriented lecture, course, or performance on campus. I pointedly asked the president if he was asking or demanding that we drop the play from our schedule. After a long pause, he said no, but he continued to raise questions. After ninety uncomfortable minutes we adjourned as he pointedly indicated that our discussion was not over.

About a week later I was summoned to the president's office, and we largely replayed our first conversation, a dialogue marked by deepening tension. At one point Ford asked what would happen if he should ask for the withdrawal of the play. Instead of answering him, I asked if he was, in fact, asking me to do so or merely applying pressure so that he did not *have* to ask. He did not reply. When this nearly two-hour meeting ended, the president indicated that we would continue the discussion. At this point, as my concern grew over Ford's intentions, I shared my version of these meetings with colleagues in the arts, all of whom immediately reacted with alarm to what was perceived as implicit pressure from the president to cancel the production.

Another meeting with the president occurred a few days later, as colleagues began to openly express concerns over what they, as well as I, considered the president's flirtation with violating academic freedom. Concern led the chair of the Humanities Division to invite the president to speak on the subject at the next division meeting, at which time he expressed his view that a public presentation was, in his estimation, not necessarily protected by the tenets of academic freedom. This caused alarm that spread through the faculty as the *Commentary* began to hammer away, devoting entire issues of its monthly publication to what in most opinions—including many conservative members of the community—were distorted, sensationalized views of the disagreement over the play's production, its content, and the intentions of everyone involved. Their efforts precipitated a flood of pro and con letters, emails, and phone calls from alumni, students and faculty, and local citizens as the controversy spread from campus publications to local and statewide newspapers. After a time tensions seemed to quiet down, but when it was learned that Ford had arranged, at great expense, for a campus panel discussion to be called "Freedom and Responsibility in the Liberal Arts" scheduled the night before the play was to open, another explosion occurred. To be dominated by national conservative figures Gertrude Himmelfarb, Michael Medved, and Dinesh D'Souza, with the liberal side represented by Jonathan Rauch and Nat Hentoff, the panel was seen by many as a preemptive strike against a production the president could not stop. Under fire for setting up the panel with no faculty involvement and receiving an angry call from Kushner himself, Ford disingenuously denied that the panel had anything to do with the play and continued to do so even after the media reported that the play was virtually the sole component of the panel's discussion. A reporter from the *Chronicle of Higher Education* arrived about three days before the opening of the production and stayed through opening night, writing a full-page story on the controversy, the panel, and the production, noting that "it did not disappoint, not even—and this is not said lightly—in comparison with the Broadway production. The 3½-hour, 26-scene performance was humorous whenever it could be, fabulous when it needed to be, moving when it should have been. It would have been an achievement at, say, New York University. At Wabash—an 824-student, all-male, liberal-arts college in a small town—it was stunning."[7]

From my first meeting with the president through the run of the play—a full year—almost every day was consumed in part with some aspect of the controversy. Responding to administrative requests for information about the play and the department's past accomplishments (apparently to prepare for questions and to justify the existence of the Theatre Department and the choice of the play for production), talking to campus publicity personnel and local press, responding to correspondence and phone calls from students, faculty, alumni, and local citizens was a distraction from preparations for a play that would be a challenge to stage in any small college theatre under the best of circumstances. All constituencies seemed to sense that, for better or worse, changes brewing in the institution were, to some extent, reflected by the production and its controversy.

Now, in the interest of full disclosure, I must "out" myself as a liberal, although I prefer the word *progressive*, and as gay-friendly, profeminist, prochoice, and a recovering Catholic. No doubt, my attraction to Kushner's play had to do, in part, with its points of connection to my personal values. But why would a director be drawn to any work, classic or contemporary, that did not connect with her or him on some personal level? Since no one at Wabash had ever challenged a play selection, I was woefully unprepared for what occurred. My lack of preparedness undoubtedly exacerbated the situation, but from the beginning it was clear that the controversy took on a life of its own. It became a catalyst for a battle over the soul of the institution that continues today, with the conflict focusing at various times on a movement toward coeducation at all-male Wabash, on efforts to recruit a more diverse faculty and student body, on greater visibility of gays and lesbians on campus, and on what one colleague currently refers to as the "onslaught of gender feminism," whatever that might be. Somehow, campus issues merged with the divisive national mood to create the conditions for an explosion, and our little production of *Millennium Approaches* was the dynamite.

Having been drawn most powerfully to the aesthetic challenges and forthrightness of the questions raised in *Angels*, I was shocked that anyone would suggest that a play should not be done because it might offend a potential donor or be seen as somehow in conflict with the institution's marketing strategy, but such views were expressed both publicly and privately. In fact, there seemed to be a range of reasons why the play was unacceptable for various constituencies. Strong language and sexual situations were most frequently cited, but it became clear that it was a perceived endorsement of the "homosexual lifestyle" and what was called the play's "liberal bias" that rankled most.

The emergence of similar controversies around the country suggested that other communities were similarly divided over *Angels in America,* as well as other plays exploring contemporary issues, including the aforementioned *Corpus Christi.* More than sixty countries saw productions of one or both parts of *Angels* during this period, as well as numerous regional and university theatres around the country. And controversy abounded at the Charlotte Repertory Theatre, Catholic University, and Kilgore College, among others. At Wabash, although the controversy made for a miserable and upsetting time, the actual work of the production and its outcomes were thrilling and reminded me of something I think I knew but had never experienced firsthand—controversy can be good. Although I would not want to go through it again, the external pressures galvanized the cast and crew, in my opinion accelerating their development as artists as they reckoned, on an individual basis, with what theatre can and should be—and what they could contribute to it.

In presenting a play exposing many of the conflicts of our divided country, I had accidentally stumbled into a teaching moment I had not envisioned. Gerald Graff writes that teaching these conflicts "has nothing to do with relativism or denying the existence of truth," as conservative critics frequently claim, and that examining and understanding the full diversity of American society could, in fact, lead to a truer sense of liberty and equality.[8]

Graff articulates a valuable model for a teaching artist and one, I believe, I had followed but had not been seriously challenged about until this controversy. For those who have personally experienced a culture wars skirmish, what I write will seem familiar, even redundant. But regardless of individual experiences, personal politics, or the articulated theatre missions, the advantage of controversy is its testing of one's beliefs and one's will to persevere when it can seem easier to step away. Even at this late date, a week does not pass without the production of *Angels* and the surrounding controversy coming up in some context for me. Controversy raises potent questions facing artists in these complex times: What is the artist's responsibility to a community? How does any theatre or arts organization articulate its mission? Who defines, dictates, and enforces community "morality" and "traditional" values? What is a truly moral (or ethical) question, and what is simply a matter of local proprieties? What strategies can be developed to turn a controversial arts event into a constructive discussion of the content of the work and the role of the arts? And, with particular emphasis on the academic community, what are my responsibilities as a teaching artist? What should guide my department in selecting plays?

The play itself taught many lessons. Kushner is a fascinating contradiction in our divided society: gay, Jewish, an artist, an intellectual, a liberal, an activist—in short, he is a living embodiment of multiple ostracized or marginalized minorities. Critics often seem uneasy writing about a contemporary American dramatist whose politics, whatever brand, are overtly expressed—and what does *that* suggest about the ability of artists to explore the terrain of morality, politics, and gender? Given that Kushner's politics fall into the "liberal" range, it is even more surprising that his work attracts acclaim and large audiences, suggesting that at the very least what we feel and what we vote may be two distinctly different things. Kushner's desire to offer theatre "that presents the world as it is, an interwoven web of the public and the private" blends fantasy, epic theatre, and realism to create a simultaneously artificial and real stage world where remarkable journeys become possible.[9] When a New York drag queen dying of AIDS meets an unhappily married Mormon woman in a mutual fever dream in *Millennium Approaches,* Kushner's merger of the real, the imagined, and the topical allows for a breaking free from the contentious impasse marking the dialogue of our times.

In *Angels,* as in most of his canon of plays and screenplays, Kushner considers the nature of morality in a nation increasingly diverse and conflicted over politics, gender, and spirituality. Here the dramatist achieves his full usefulness in framing the unresolved—and perhaps unresolvable—questions before us as a society, including the central ones: What is moral? Are we a moral nation? Can we constructively embrace the inevitability of change as we move into the future? Is America rushing toward apocalypse, or is it bound for a brighter tomorrow? Kushner, a cautious, questioning optimist, is acutely aware that there are no easy answers or simple endings, but he insists that the possibility of, and the hope for, change, justice, and moral progress is always possible if we can break away from the rigid, calcified conservative-versus-liberal positions that separate us. And he insists that the artist bears a profound responsibility to explore these questions and to push us forward as a society.

Angels is a moral call to arms and gives form to the reasons I was drawn into a life in the theatre in the first place and the reasons I stay in it and choose, through teaching, to strive to awaken my students to the power of drama aimed at inspiring moral debate. Can we find ways to live together in mutual respect and concern despite our differences? And what could be more moral than facing that question?

In my opinion culture wars controversies have led to outcomes few artists caught up in the heat of the debate have had time to notice. The censorious are losing most of these skirmishes, and they are likely to lose the war. Artists should worry less about controversy, despite the potential, and often real, financial risks, as well as the exhaustion resulting from fighting these battles. In fact, one might argue, artists owe a debt of gratitude, however ironic this may seem, to the assailants of free expression. Mean-spirited, personal, and potentially violent attacks can stiffen resolve aimed at creating strategies to support work vulnerable to the withdrawal of federal, state, and local funding. Artists can also be empowered by the genuine and heartening support of the public in response to censorious assaults.

Engaging a community in the arts—and, more important, in the human, social, political, moral, and religious issues raised—should be an artist's goal. Artists show a community to itself, they illuminate other cultures and strategies of existence, and, most important, they invite a community to face complex issues, creating an opportunity to reevaluate moral standards. This, I would submit, is worth the cost of controversy to all sides.

We need to develop tougher hides in doing our work unapologetically, despite the often virulent and sometimes surreal censorious aggression. I failed in this because I took much of it personally. The lack of institutional support and trust, and what seemed personal betrayals in my professional home, hurt. Which leads me to suggest that those of us who make art must vigorously support artists targeted for this sort of harassment. To that end artists must also talk about their work. This is difficult for me; as a theatre director I have always believed that what was on the stage should speak for itself. Attempting to explain work, sometimes even before I have done it, risks minimizing and flattening it. I believed it was for others to interpret, debate, celebrate, or criticize what they saw, but my encounter with controversy changed my mind about this. We must explain our work and our mission to the community, and we must challenge those who would censor. If they are brought into the light of debate—and I may be too optimistic—they almost certainly will not prevail.

We must assert that it should be the responsibility of government to support art that aims to enlarge horizons and challenge preconceptions. Artists must also go further; we must depend less on governmental or institutional funds, even if we believe—rightly—that a civilized society should support the creation of art for the sake of our cultural souls. We need to strive for the election of candidates prepared to view art as central to the well-being of a society.

Controversy is not pleasant for those working in the arts. Bomb scares, threatened and actual withdrawal of funding, pickets, hate mail, obscene phone calls, media feeding frenzies, and personal ridicule—all of which occurred in my culture wars skirmish—seem to regularly accompany the presentation of controversial work. Each hysterical outburst can have the constructive result of causing the public to reflect more on the motives of the censorious than on those of the artist whose work is assailed.

There is no denying that these are difficult times for all artists—we are blamed for lowering moral standards, for desecrating religion, and for inspiring violence (this last is mostly directed at film and television). When we appropriately lament violence and the perceived moral decline in our society, can we really think that controversial art is *more* responsible than the obvious culprits of economic, racial, and gender injustice, corporate greed, and political opportunism? Artists exist, in part, to offer a vision of compassion and redemption; to move society toward a more humane outlook that is less interested in guns than in art, more inclined toward giving than taking, and believes in a more inclusive brand of family values than that which is espoused on the campaign trail. Artists unafraid of controversy make for a good start toward a truly moral society; certainly it is not enough, but it is a start.

In making a moral journey as an artist, Kushner is guided by what he calls "a pessimism of the intellect" and "an optimism of the will."[10] He continues to focus on those lessons of the past that follow us into the future, and he does so with the realization that "much has changed in such an incredibly short time."[11] Change *is* possible; in fact, it is necessary, and, looking ahead as any true progressive must, Kushner sees us spinning forward into an unknown future that, despite our deep cultural discontents, may be imagined as a truly moral place, a society driven by hope and compassion.

Notes

1. Tony Kushner, "Fighting the Art Bullies," *Nation*, Nov. 29, 1999, 41.
2. Ibid.

3. Patrick J. Buchanan, "1992 Republican National Convention Speech," Aug. 17, 1992, www.buchanan.org/pa-920817-rnc.html.

4. Allan Bloom, *The Closing of the American Mind* (New York: Simon and Schuster, 1987), 202.

5. See Lawrence W. Levine, *The Opening of the American Mind: Canons, Culture, and History* (New York: Beacon Press, 1996).

6. See Jane Alexander, *Command Performance: An Actress in the Theatre of Politics* (Washington, DC: Public Affairs Press, 2000).

7. Lawrence Biemiller, "*Angels in America* Challenges Students at Wabash College," Notes from Academe, *Chronicle of Higher Education,* Oct. 18, 1996, B2.

8. Gerald Graff, *Beyond the Culture Wars: How Teaching the Conflicts Can Revitalize American Education* (New York: Norton, 1992), 15.

9. Tony Kushner, "Notes about a Political Theatre," *Kenyon Review* 19, nos. 3–4 (summer/fall 1997): 22.

10. See Jane Edwardes, "Kabul's Eye," *Time Out,* June 30–July 7, 1999, n.p.

11. Ibid.

Excerpt from the Symposium Response

Steve Scott

OKAY, THANK YOU ... ANY QUESTIONS? [laughter] As I was just moaning to everyone this morning, this conference has been both exhausting and exhilarating. In my line of work, as I just said outside, we don't have staff meetings to talk about theatre and "moral order," but we do have staff meetings to talk about budgeting and how we're going to sell the goddamn show to the goddamn audiences and all of that. So it's interesting to bring these kinds of theoretical questions into some of the practical spheres that I deal with every day.

And forgive me if I don't go through and kind of distill each of the presentations; I am thinking more about the questions raised by the presentations, and from a very selfish point of view, i.e., "how does all of this affect *me,* and how am *I* processing all of this?"

I found, actually this morning, I found a couple of statements that were made in different presentations that distill the basic tensions that I think we're all dealing with. In Mr. [Nicholas] Dekker's paper, he at one point, in the discussion of the Edwardian pack of managers, and their attempts to make the theatre "respectable," said "respectability equals morality"—if in no other way but through dress codes and etiquette codes and other outward shows. There is certainly a tension between that and the thing that Ian [MacLennan] pointed out in the last paper on cross-dressing at the Globe, that "the more an act is done, the less of an impact it has." And I thought David [Carlyon] had a fascinating point in his presentation on William Dunlap yesterday, about how we, even as theatre artists and theatre scholars and theatre people, are sometimes afraid of our own theatrical impulses, that we strive in some ways to antitheatricalize our own theatricalization. As we keep talking about audiences and audience response, it seems that the basic tension throughout the history of our art form has been between the rational and the irrational creative impulse; the impulse that causes us to tell stories or to try to get at other feelings of creation and how scary that can be for us and for our audiences.

We've talked about censorship and how the kinds of things that are not or were not considered to be "respectable" tend to be based on sexual impulses. In our discussion of the NEA controversy yesterday it was interesting that it boiled down to projects that deal with human sexuality and different expressions of human sexuality. And, of course, sexuality and theatrical creation come from exactly the same place—scary, unknowable, and uncontrollable in some ways, even to us. So I don't know where to go with that tension because it's the tension that I've, I think, been exploring since I was old enough to realize what that tension was, and I think it's something that we all try to negotiate. But I found that the question that echoed through presentation after presentation after presentation was "how do we rationalize what is essentially an irrational act?" . . . that is, an essentially irrational thing? Even in the act of explaining, as we all were attempting to do this weekend, we must ask, how can we explain those things that are inexplicable? And I'm thinking about in my own life, about the whole idea of the antitheatrical, and how we rush to examine our own theatrical impulses and, in some ways, to rationalize and tamp them down. Even in the practice of the theatre as business, when I'm dealing with my board, my job is not to be the free artistic being that I am in the rehearsal room; my job is to sit down in my business suit and explain to businessmen how what we do is important and necessary and all of that stuff. So this question resonated with me in a number of different ways.

Coming back again to the role and responsibility of the artist in initiating the dialogue: in one of the discussions we got into on Friday night, we asked about how much responsibility the artist has for making that dialogue happen. How much responsibility does the artist have for providing a platform for dialogue, for bringing the audience into that, and then making the audience comfortable with that dialogue? And from a very practical viewpoint, then, what is an effective response by an artist to controversy? What is an effective response to attacks from the right, or the left, or just from our own audiences? Mac Wellman sending scripts to Jesse Helms is great, but does that really, *really* attack the problem, or is it just a kind of "nyah-nyah-nyah . . . I wrote a dirty play so here you are!"?

And also because I work in an institution, I must ask about the role of individual artists and their relationships and responsibilities to the institutions that employ them. Where does the institution take over? How proprietary does the institution become with respect to the artist? It was interesting when we explored that question with respect to Sarah Kane's work yesterday, about the role that the Royal Court has continued to have in the championing, sponsoring, and marketing of Sarah Kane. Sarah Kane is theirs. And since Sarah Kane is now dead, she will always be theirs. And I keep thinking of all the theatres that do new work and how frequently we have that relationship with the writers that we champion. Every theatre I know of does, but does such a proprietary relationship begin to distort what the artist is really doing with his or her work? I don't know.

Another interesting point arose in Susan [Kattwinkel]'s paper: how does morality become a marketing tool? How does the marketing of a "respectable" experience render what we do on our stages as "safe"? As I told Susan, she could now be the marketing director of the Goodman Theatre because she has experience with that.

Also, one of things that I found fascinating yesterday in some of the papers was the depiction of "the Other"—when we were talking about "poor white trash" and the depiction of the Appalachian figure in mainstream plays. This has been an ongoing discussion, obviously, for every ethnic and cultural group: how the mainstream depicts ethnic experience. Certainly the African American experience was not depicted in any realistic way until after African American artists began telling their own stories. How does the mainstream theatre deal with "the Other" until such time as "the Other" is empowered enough to tell his or her own story?

I was also intrigued by the whole discussion about "lower" and "higher" forms of entertainment—and how NASCAR kept coming up! I think NASCAR is actually an art unto itself, but there is this feeling that "low" entertainment and "high" art are two very different things. Is there an intersection? And if so, how do these two categories inform each other? Is it an intersection that might lead to bringing more people into the artistic experience? Again, I don't know.

And the whole idea of classism in American theatre—we talk about racism, we talk about sexism, we talk about gender bias, we talk about all sorts of *-isms,* but I have found that in much of the work that we have produced, classism is now the most incendiary issue, that it seems to be a pervading through-line in much of our discussion. America does not like to see itself as a classist society. Actually, we would rather see ourselves as racist than classist, I suspect, in some ways, although that is a gross generalization. But I know the plays that we at Goodman have done that have attacked classism have been much more controversial than the plays that we have done that have dealt with racism, which is a fairly acceptable *-ism* to examine. So, again, these are just questions. I tend to respond to questions with questions (maybe because I have no real sense of myself, I don't know).

We look at all these things in a historical context, but what's important to me is to learn from that historical context those things that we can apply to what we are doing today—as artists, as teachers, as practitioners—this is what really resonates for me. So how does what happened in the Edwardian era reflect how we conduct our business, the business of our theatre institutions, today? How does the whole idea of the women performers in the "Leg Shows" (and how they were described in moralistic terms) relate to how we position artists today as morally and ethically responsible members of society rather than free spirits who have tapped into a kind of unnamable, indefinable, and somewhat frightening impulse?

So that's where I ended up: I thought it was fascinating because it made me think about a lot of things that I don't necessarily think about on a daily basis. I would be very interested to hear your responses to this response in terms of trying to contextualize all of the things that we have talked about in the past forty-eight hours. It's only been two days—but my God!—I feel like I've been here for a month, and I don't want to go back to Chicago because the weather has been good.

Contributors

Rosemarie K. Bank has published in *Theatre Journal, Nineteenth-Century Theatre, Theatre History Studies, Essays in Theatre, Theatre Research International, Modern Drama, Journal of Dramatic Theory and Criticism, Women in American Theatre, Feminist Rereadings of Modern American Drama, The American Stage, Critical Theory and Performance, Performing America,* and *Of Borders and Thresholds.* She is the author of *Theatre Culture in America, 1825–1860* (New York: Cambridge University Press, 1997); and is currently preparing *Staging the Native, 1792–1892*. Several times a Fellow of the National Endowment for the Humanities, she was editor of *Theatre Survey* from 2000 to 2003 and currently serves on the editorial boards of three scholarly journals in theatre. She is professor of theatre and coordinator of graduate studies at Kent State University.

David Carlyon, an independent scholar, is the author of *Dan Rice: The Most Famous Man You've Never Heard Of,* featured in the *New York Times* and on C-SPAN's *Booknotes.* He's published in *Theatre Symposium, New England Theatre Journal, Theatre Topics,* and *American Theatre* and had a play produced at Theatre Virginia. After obtaining a Northwestern PhD, he became an assistant professor at the University of Michigan at Flint. He gives master classes in acting, including Carnegie-Mellon, and is a stage movement consultant, recently at Goodspeed. A graduate of the law school at Berkeley, he has been a forest-fire fighter, a military policeman, and a Ringling Brothers and Barnum & Bailey Circus clown.

Eileen Curley is an assistant professor of English at Marist College in Poughkeepsie, New York, where she teaches dramatic literature and designs scenery. She received her PhD in theatre history, theory, and literature at Indiana University. Her current research focuses on nineteenth-century amateur theatricals in the United States and the United Kingdom, although her interests also include classical antiquity, the British Restoration, and theatrical architecture and audiences.

James Fisher, professor of theatre at Wabash College, has authored several books, including *The Theater of Tony Kushner: Living Past Hope* (New York: Routledge, 2001) and the forthcoming *Historical Dictionary of the American Theater: Modernism, 1880–1930* (Jefferson, NC: McFarland, 2007), coauthoring with Felicia Hardison Londré. He has published articles in numerous periodicals and held several research fellowships. Fisher edits *The Puppetry Yearbook* (now in its sixth volume) and the recent *Tony Kushner: New Essays on the Art and Politics of the Plays* (Jefferson, NC: McFarland, 2006). Fisher was McLain-McTurnan-Arnold Research Scholar at Wabash and named "Indiana Theatre Person of the Year" by the Indiana Theatre Association in 1997.

Roger Freeman is assistant professor of theatre at Rochester Institute of Technology in Rochester, New York. His chief research interests are in narrative structure and the influence of electronic media on playwriting and performance conventions. He has presented at the Comparative Drama Conference, the Association for Theatre in Higher Education Conference, the Midwest Modern Language Association Conference, the Twentieth-Century Literature Conference, and the Southwest Popular Culture Conference and has published in the *Journal of Dramatic Theory and Criticism.* He holds a PhD from Ohio State University.

John W. Frick is professor of theatre and American studies at the University of Virginia. He is the author of *Theatre, Culture, and Temperance Reform in Nineteenth-Century America* (New York: Cambridge University Press, 2003); *New York's First Theatrical Center: The Rialto at Union Square* (Ann Arbor: University of Michigan Research Press, 1985); and coeditor, with Carlton Ward, of *The Directory of Historic American Theatres and Theatrical Directors: A Biographical Dictionary* (New York: Greenwood, 1987). Professor Frick is president of the American Theatre and Drama Society.

Leah Lowe is assistant professor of theater at Connecticut College. Her research interests include gender issues in narrative comedy and nineteenth-century American entertainment. She received her MFA in directing from the University of Minnesota and her PhD from Florida State University.

Rachel Rusch is currently completing her doctorate at the Yale School of Drama, where she is an Andrew W. Mellon Foundation Dissertation Research Fellow. She is the associate editor of *Theater Magazine* and a former teaching fellow at Yale College.

Steve Scott has been associate producer at the Goodman Theatre since 1987, where he has overseen more than 150 productions. Mr. Scott has served on advisory panels for the Chicago Office of Fine Arts, the Illinois Arts Council, the National Endowment for the Arts, and the Pew Charitable Trust/Philadelphia Theatre Initiative; he currently serves as an NEA site evaluator and a member of the Jeff Committee's Artistic and Technical Team, as well as a board member for Season of Concern. He is an artistic associate of the About Face Theatre, a member of the Eclipse Theatre ensemble, and one of six resident directors for WBEZ's Stories on Stage. Mr. Scott is also a faculty member at Act One Studio and received the Award of Honor from the Illinois Theatre Association. In addition, he is a contributor to the recently published *Encyclopedia of Chicago*.